Cherry
Blossom
Winter

Cherry
Blossom
Winter

Jennifer Maruno

DUNDURN
TORONTO

Editor: Cheryl Hawley
Design: Jesse Hooper
Printer: Webcom

Library and Archives Canada Cataloguing in Publication

Maruno, Jennifer, 1950-
     Cherry blossom winter / Jennifer Maruno.

Issued also in electronic formats.
ISBN 978-1-4597-0211-0

     1. Japanese Canadians--Evacuation and relocation, 1942-1945--Juvenile fiction. I. Title.

PS8626.A785C54 2012   jC813'.6   C2011-908025-7

1   2   3   4   5   16   15   14   13   12

 Conseil des Arts Canada Council
du Canada for the Arts   Canadä    ONTARIO ARTS COUNCIL
CONSEIL DES ARTS DE L'ONTARIO

We acknowledge the support of the **Canada Council for the Arts** and the **Ontario Arts Council** for our publishing program. We also acknowledge the financial support of the **Government of Canada** through the **Canada Book Fund** and **Livres Canada Books**, and the **Government of Ontario** through the **Ontario Book Publishing Tax Credit** and the **Ontario Media Development Corporation**.

Printed and bound in Canada.

VISIT US AT
Dundurn.com | Definingcanada.ca | @dundurnpress | Facebook.com/dundurnpress

Dundurn
3 Church Street, Suite 500
Toronto, Ontario, Canada
M5E 1M2

Gazelle Book Services Limited
White Cross Mills
High Town, Lancaster, England
LA1 4XS

Dundurn
2250 Military Road
Tonawanda, NY
U.S.A. 14150

For Erin Jane Travis

Chapter One

APRIL 1943

"Michiko," her mother called up the back staircase, "please come down."

Michiko put down the piece of paper she was trying to fold and glanced at her little brother's body curled on the sofa. Looking at his bowl-shaped hair she wondered how much longer he would sleep. Should she leave her *origami* or take it with her?

"Michiko," Mrs. Minagawa called out louder with hint of impatience.

It must be important, Michiko thought. Her mother was not the type to raise her voice.

"Coming," she replied. She lifted the pillow of the chair and placed the half-folded paper beneath it, hoping Hiro wouldn't wake and find it. She raced down the steep back stairs of the drugstore. As she skipped across the black-and-white squares of linoleum, she gave each one of the red stools in front of the soda bar a spin. Three rows of sparkling ice-cream glasses waited in front of the mirrored wall.

Two women stood with her mother beside the cash register. The younger was pretty in a pale, bony way. The bobbing bunch of brown curls on top of her head fascinated Michiko. Even if she twisted a lock of her hair around her finger as hard as she could, it would always slip right back into straightness.

"Michiko," her mother said, "these ladies would like to see what you are wearing."

"What?" Michiko asked.

Her mother frowned.

"I mean, pardon me?" she said in a softer voice.

The women smiled. Their faces told Michiko they were probably mother and daughter.

The younger woman waved her hand about in a circular motion. "Turn around, Michiko," she said. "Show us your dress."

Michiko twirled in the candy-striped cotton dress with large, deep pockets that her mother had made for her tenth birthday. The skirt spun like a top.

The older women caught the hem. She wore light grey, skin-tight kid gloves that closed with a tiny pearl button.

Michiko noticed there were little holes along the seams and the button on the other glove was missing.

The woman examined her mother's tiny perfect stitches. "Your work is so fine," she said. "The stitches are difficult to see." She let it drop.

Her mother smoothed Hiro's car coat out on the counter. The younger woman examined the small hood and felt her way down the sleeves.

"That's my brother's coat," Michiko informed them. "My mother made it from my father's old one." Looking at it, she realized how much her brother had grown since leaving Vancouver.

Both women nodded.

"We make do with what we have," Michiko's mother said.

Eiko Minigawa was the master of making do. She recycled, remodelled, and repaired everything. When they moved into the apartment she washed the empty rice bags in bleach and hung them in the sun to make rice-bag curtains. She then took down the apartment curtains and made each of them a blouse. The blackout material from Vancouver became her father's shirt.

"That's exactly why we are here," said the older woman. "Edna Morrison told us your mother is the finest seamstress she has ever known."

Eiko put her fingertips to her lips. With her other hand she waved away the compliment.

"Mrs. Morrison is right," Michiko said. "Did she tell you about the quilt?" Michiko turned to her mother. But her mother flashed her eyes and shook her head.

Michiko had forgotten — she wasn't to suppose to discuss the quilt with anyone outside of the family. But she wanted to brag how clever her mother had been to fill the squares with paper money. All of their savings came with them before the government closed the Japanese banks.

A bang at the back of the store made them all turn. Michiko's father, Sam Minigawa, staggered in under the weight of several cardboard boxes. Michiko ran to hold the door.

"Can I offer you a cup of tea upstairs?" Eiko said to the two women, moving out from behind the counter. "It is black," she added, knowing that they probably wouldn't appreciate the tiny green sticks and leaves of *cha*, as her family did.

"That would be lovely," the older woman said in a whispery voice. "I could do with a nice cup of tea." She turned to Michiko and gave a smile that crinkled the fine skin around her pale watery eyes. "Thank you very much, young lady."

Michiko watched them pass. There was no clothing store in town and if you bought from the Eaton's catalogue you looked like everyone else. The women would talk about dressmaking and look at patterns. Best of all, they would be upstairs when her little brother awoke. Now that Hiro was walking, he was *yancha*: very naughty.

Her father dropped the boxes at one end of the counter. He removed a small folding knife from his back pocket and cut the string. Michiko knew he would add it to the ever-growing spool that he kept under the counter. Right now it was the size of a baseball.

"Ready to help?" he asked with a smile.

This was Michiko's favourite part about living above the drugstore. Not only did she sleep above a soda fountain, she got to help stock the shelves.

Geechan, her grandfather, came in next from his morning walk. He rested his hand-carved stick against the wall. With it he poked under hedges and pushed aside branches and grass. Her grandfather never returned empty-handed. Michiko loved the fleshy fan-shaped mushrooms, the tight green, hairy coils everyone called fiddleheads, and the wild strawberries he collected from the woods. Today his brown weathered hands carried several small wooden pegs.

Geechan removed his large black rubber boots and slipped into well-worn woven slippers. He shuffled toward them, rubbing his hands and grinning. "Comics come?" he asked. They were the only things he read these days, since Japanese newspapers were forbidden.

"No comics today," Sam replied. He turned to Michiko. "Looks like Geechan will have to wait a little longer for *Popeye the Sailor Man*." He carried one of the boxes over to the magazine rack. "Personally, I like *Joe Palooka*."

Michiko smiled. It was wonderful to have her father back with them. Just before her ninth birthday, the government sent him away. All men born in Japan had to go far from the coast. He didn't talk a lot about working in the mountains of Alberta, building roads, but she knew he didn't get a lot to eat and was always cold.

Their whole life changed because of the stupid war. It made her burn with indignation when she thought about it. Her mother, baby brother, aunt, and grandfather had to leave Vancouver just because they were Japanese. They were lucky to rent a farmhouse. Most people slept in tents waiting for the government to build them a tiny wooden house. So many Japanese families came into this small town that Japanese children had to attend school in three places.

A small fist rapped at the drugstore window. "Here is our *Kairanban* girl," Michiko called out, unlocking the front door. "Right on time."

The small brass bell over the door jingled. Mr. Hayashi stood behind Kiko.

Kiko, a short, pudgy girl, placed a small stack of *Kairanban* on the counter. Her flat nose sat on her face like a button. Kiko once told Michiko she pinched it every day to make it point.

Michiko had met Kiko Sagara at the Hardware Store School. She sat next to her with her arms crossed, hands tucked under her armpits, glaring at the teacher. Kiko didn't want to be back in class after a whole year of freedom. It was Kiko who taught Michiko new ways to fold paper. She helped Michiko find the right paper for her tulips.

"Put them behind the counter," Mr. Hayashi directed. "A newspaper written in *Kanji* makes some people in town nervous." This short man, full of energy, respected and admired by all, knew the rules. As camp security officer he translated for those who didn't understand.

"They probably think it's something subversive," Sam said.

"The only thing subversive is Mrs. Takata's recipe for meatless meatloaf," he replied, and gave a great hearty laugh.

"Can you stay?" Michiko asked.

"Of course," Kiko replied. "My father knows there's no point in asking me to rush back from your house." She smiled through the curtain of straight dark hair that covered her eyes. Kiko didn't have a mother to show her how to use a bobby pin or barrette.

"I have a secret," Kiko whispered in Michiko's ear.

"Tell me at the pond," Michiko told her. "I'm going to look for frogs."

"You mean tadpoles," Kiko corrected her. "They won't be frogs until summer." Having a newspaper editor for a father, Kiko was always sure of her facts.

Together they filled the magazine rack. The specialness of the day filled Michiko with joy. What could be better than having a friend like Kiko ready to share a secret?

Chapter Two

THE SECRET

Michiko waited at the top of the landing while Kiko removed her shoes. It took time to loosen the laces in the thick piece of brown leather that rode their shoes like a saddle. Both of them desperately wanted a pair of black patent Mary Janes from the catalogue.

Kiko slipped her feet into a pair of woven-grass slippers on the landing.

"Can Kiko stay for lunch?" Michiko asked. Her mother stood with her back to them, stirring a pot at the stove.

"Hello, Mrs. Minagawa," Kiko said in a quiet voice. "If there's not enough, I understand."

"We have enough," Michiko's mother said as she added slivers of mushroom to the tiny bits of chopped meat cooking in *shoyu*. "You are welcome to stay." Steam rose from the rice pot simmering on the stove. Its butter-like smell filled the kitchen.

"Can we help?" Kiko asked.

Michiko groaned. Kiko was always trying to please her mother.

"You can help me by taking Hiro outside for some fresh air," Eiko told them. "I can work faster if I don't have to keep an eye on him."

Geechan sat at the kitchen table, wrapping twine around the pegs. Soon Michiko's Uncle Ted would come to help them dig a garden. Ted was the first member of the Minagawa family to arrive in this town. He used to build boats, but the government sent him there to build little wooden houses instead. When they moved to the apartment, Ted filled the farmhouse with bunks. All the single men lived there now and they called it the Bachelor House.

~ ~ ~

Even though the town still wore a bleak winter look, the trees along the main street had a haze of new growth. Michiko hoped they could plant flowers. Fresh flowers would bring a smile to her mother's face. She loved to watch her mother use her short sharp scissors. After clipping a bloom, she would wind it with wire and stick it into a cluster of pins at the bottom of a vase.

Michiko, Kiko, and Hiro stepped off the wooden walkway in front of the drugstore onto Main Street, which ran from the mountains to the lake.

Two streets divided Main Street into three parts. Church Street crossed at the top, where houses surrounded the little white steeple church. These small frame houses with narrow windows were different from the ones in Vancouver. There weren't any shingled sides or verandahs with pillars.

Maple Street crossed Main in the middle. This block held the butcher shop and the drugstore where Michiko lived. Across the street was the Hardware Store School.

The Mounted Police office, the General Store, the Hall, and a few empty stores were at the lower end of town. Boards covered many of the upper windows and piles of dirty snow and dead leaves hung about the doorways. The post office was inside the General Store. Across from the General Store, huge wooden steps led to the Grand Hotel's waterfront.

The national flag stirred lightly in the breeze above the hotel, the only three-storey building in town. On the street level, beneath the wide wooden verandah, were dim hotel offices. The entrance hall off the verandah led into a long hall with rooms on either side. These were the classrooms for high school students. The top floor bedrooms housed the women teachers. Michiko's Aunt Sadie was one of the teachers at the Hotel High School.

Michiko and Kiko walked Hiro down the street to the baseball field. It was really just the vacant lot beside the hotel, but the kids used it as a playground. A large pond sat in the middle.

Halfway across the field, Kiko turned to the Mounted Police station and stuck out her tongue. Michiko raised her eyebrows. "Why did you do that?"

"Because," Kiko answered, "those Mounties are going to make us move again."

"When?" Michiko asked. She tried not to think about what had happened to her father because whenever she did she got scared.

"Who knows?" Kiko responded. "All I know is my father is calling a meeting."

"Is that your secret?" Michiko asked as Hiro broke away from their hands and ran across the field. "That there will be a meeting?"

"No." Kiko giggled. "This is something fun, not something pol-it-i-cal."

Michiko had to smile at the way Kiko dragged out every one of the syllables. It was an imitation of her father's way of speaking.

Hiro picked up a stick and gave one of the small puddles a poke. The ice made the stick bend and snap. Hiro discarded the stick and picked up a small rock. He threw the rock into the middle of the puddle, making a spiderweb crack. The girls joined him, breaking the ice with their heels. The strong stench of mud made them plug their noses.

Hiro investigated another slab of ice. He picked up a rock and threw it down. Michiko saw him frown when it bounced and skidded away. This gave her an idea.

"Hiro," she called out, "we can slide the rocks."

With the inside of her foot, Michiko shot the rock at him. Then she moved her legs apart.

"Shoot it in between my legs," she said.

"He shoots, he scores!" a tall boy called out as he walked toward them. He had a nose full of freckles and bright blue-green eyes with lashes that were almost invisible. Tufts of golden hair stuck out from his green toque.

Kiko clutched Michiko's arm as he approached. Her eyes filled with anxiety.

"Hi, Clarence," Michiko said to the tall lanky boy. She wasn't surprised to see him. He often walked into town along the railroad tracks. Michiko gave him a big smile.

Hiro grinned and put his arms up in the air when the boy approached. Clarence picked him up and swung him around. "You should be playing baseball," he said putting him down.

Clarence searched the ground for a thick stick. He showed Hiro how to toss a rock in the air and hit it. Hiro gave it a swipe but missed.

Michiko turned to Kiko. "This is Clarence," she said. Clarence was the only kid in town who made friends with her when she arrived. "Clarence, this is Kiko Sagara."

"Where are you going?" Kiko asked.

"Your place," Clarence responded. "Ma sent me out for soap." His face puckered, making all his freckles mash together. "She's dragged out the tin tub and is making everyone take a bath, now that the weather is nice."

"My father will be happy to sell you soap," Michiko told him. "You'll be the one person who doesn't want soya sauce."

"Doesn't your house have a bathtub?" Kiko asked as she looked him up and down. "I thought everyone in town had a bathtub."

Michiko knew that Clarence lived in a small wooden house with a corrugated iron roof and a little grey shed out back for a toilet, like the houses in the orchard. She was grateful she no longer had to follow the hard-packed path to the outhouse they had to use on the farm. She remembered what it was like sitting on the cold porcelain seat, fighting off spiders.

Clarence shook his head. "I don't live in town."

"Me neither," said Kiko. "Our tub is so small you can only put one foot in at a time."

Michiko changed the subject. She couldn't help feeling guilty that she had a toilet with a pull handle, bathtub, and plenty of hot water. "What we need," she said, "is a swim. Then we can all get clean at the same time."

"That's so funny you said that," Kiko said, clapping her hands together. "That's my secret. The men in the orchard are going to build an *ofuro*!"

Chapter Three

THE GARDEN

"There won't be any work done on a bathhouse until everyone has put in their garden," Sam told the family when Michiko shared the news at dinner.

He was right. Everyone in the orchard hoped to harvest a few vegetables before the next winter. They spent April slashing away the crabgrass and thistles in order to plant their small patch of land. From dawn to dusk they bent over the hard soil hoeing. Then they carted water from the ground tap at the end of each street.

Geechan spent the mild spring days wandering the lakeshore, creek bed, and forest paths collecting rocks. He especially liked the ones with rainbow colours.

"Ashi o kiosukete kudasai," he muttered every time a rock thudded to the ground at the back of the drugstore. Michiko heard him say it often as she took the sheets from the line.

"Why does Geechan tell the rocks to take care of their feet?" she asked her mother when she took a basket of dry linen inside. "Doesn't he mean watch out for his toes?"

Her mother lifted a sheet from the basket. "He's speaking to his invisible plant," Eiko said with a smile. "Once he has a large circle of stones he will fill it with soil and make a garden." She folded the sheet. "He knows if you plant by rocks, vegetables will grow faster. The rocks catch the sun and keep plant roots warm."

~ ~ ~

A sound like a giant knife scraping across toast made Michiko hop out of bed and look out her bedroom window. The early morning sun spilled across the yard. As usual, Geechan was up and working before anyone else. Michiko watched him drag his hoe across the ground. Then he lifted it in the air and brought it down hard. The ground broke. He scraped, lifted, and broke the ground a second time. In this rhythmic pattern, Geechan worked his way from the back of the garden to the front. Then he paused, removed a handkerchief from his back pocket, leaned on the hoe, and mopped his brow.

Michiko put on knee socks that no longer came up to her knee, blue drill pants that had been let down twice, and a navy sweater with patches across the elbows. By the time she ate breakfast and pulled on her rubber boots, the first long furrow of broken soil waited. She watched a robin land. He cocked his head to the ground. Then he pulled a soft worm from the ground and flew away.

"What's this row going to be?" Michiko asked.

Geechan shrugged and made his way to the back of the garden to start again.

"I hope we are putting in potatoes," Clarence announced, appearing from the side of the building. A burlap sack swung at his side as he walked. He wore a flannel shirt and denim pants with a small hole in one of the knees. Thick striped socks topped his scuffed hob-nailed boots. "I just love potatoes."

"What's in the bag?" Michiko asked. She was pleased Clarence remembered to come.

"I made three of them," Clarence announced proudly, "one for you, Hiro, and me." He placed the sack at Michiko's feet.

"They just look like cans to me," Michiko said, opening the sack and peering inside.

"They are cans." Clarence pulled one out and showed her the rows of small holes in the bottom. "They're watering cans. You dip it in the bucket and move it along the row."

"Good thinking," Ted commented, striding into the yard. He shouldered a shovel, pickaxe, and hoe, his strong carpenter hands clamped over their wooden handles. His open shirt revealed a snow-white undershirt. His deep black eyes sparkled.

"Something for each of us," Ted said, letting the tools clatter to the ground. "You pick."

"I pick the pick," Clarence said. "I've always wanted to strike gold like a prospector."

"You mean silver," Michiko corrected. "This used to be silver town, not gold."

"This town is nothing but a ghost town now," Ted said as he lifted the shovel.

"Don't forget to plant peonies for prosperity," Michiko's Aunt Sadie called out to them from the back door. She put the red-painted tips of her long straight fingers to her lips and blew Michiko a kiss. Hiro, in her arms, played with the pompons dangling from her sweater.

Looking at her mother's elegant sister, most people would think Sadie was too *haikara* for hard work. But when they first arrived she had chopped wood, hauled water, and scrubbed clothes just like everyone else. If anyone needed help, she would be the first to put on her overalls.

"Hiro, what do you think we should plant?" Michiko asked with a grin.

"A beanstalk," Ted replied. "That way he can climb it." Then he added under his breath, *"Yancha kozo de ne."*

Michiko giggled. Sadie said Ted was just as mischievous when he was a boy.

"For Hiro," Sadie said walking into the garden, "we can plant an iris."

"Why?" asked Clarence.

"Our mother was forever trying to grow a Hirohito iris, but it would not bloom."

"We better plant more than flowers," Ted muttered in exasperation. "Especially if we have a winter like the last one."

Ted, Clarence, and Michiko helped Geechan dig and scrape the soil until the rectangular patch of land was full of scalloped edged rows.

"Tomorrow we sow," Ted announced. "Each person gets to plant a row." He reached out for the pickaxe from Clarence. "You get to do the potatoes," he said, ruffling the boy's bright red hair with his hand.

Clarence waved and headed home. The rest went indoors for lunch. Any other time Clarence would be welcome to stay, but not today. Today the family had important business.

The night before, someone pounding on the shop door had made everyone stop eating in surprise. Michiko watched her father place his napkin at the side of his plate and rise from the dinner table. They all stared at the grey envelope he returned with, wondering what it was, but Sam did not open it. He put it down next to his plate, tapped it lightly, and said, "We wait for Ted."

Later that night Michiko turned the letter over. The words OPENED BY CENSOR and the examiner number were missing. Michiko hoped it meant they could go back to Vancouver.

Her mother spread the tablecloth and set out the napkins. Eiko always insisted their table be set properly. "It makes the food taste better," she said many times.

Michiko waited patiently for their lunch to finish.

Finally her father took a knife, slit open the envelope, and handed the letter to Ted.

Ted scanned the letter. Taking a deep breath he read it out loud: "Please be informed that your property, in its course of sale, received a price equal to that placed upon it by an independent appraiser."

Her mother folded her hands in her lap and said, "I should think so. We painted and installed new furnace pipes."

Michiko jumped into the conversation. "We had a garden in the back and in the front." She stopped talking when Sadie looked her in the eye and shook her head.

"Proceeds will not be given to the owners," Ted continued as his voice grew low, "unless they can prove need."

Sadie gave a sharp incredulous cry.

Ted lowered the letter to the table. "You don't want to hear the rest."

Eiko buried her face in her hands. "What do they mean by need?" she said.

"Let me see that," Sadie said, snatching up the letter. She scanned it quickly with her eyes, and then read out loud, "Your Ford was sold by the government for thirty-three dollars. Handling charges for the transaction were thirty dollars." Her voice moved to anger as she shouted out the words: "We will forward you a cheque in the amount of three dollars."

Sadie waved the letter in front of everyone's face. "Do you mean to tell me that you can't get the price of your own house or your own car? All you get is three measly dollars?"

Ted took the letter from her and handed it back to Sam. "You knew the house sold."

Geechan patted Sam's arm. "We can never see the sun rise by looking into the west."

"How can you say that?" Sadie screeched. "First they take your boat, then our radios and cameras." She stood up, shoving her chair behind her. "They forced Sam into a chain gang," she exclaimed, "and all you can say is, look the other way?"

Michiko held her breath, expecting her grandfather to rise and rebuke Sadie. But he didn't.

Sadie threw the letter to the table. "I will never stop looking back." She strode out of the kitchen, down the stairs, and slammed the back door.

No one at the table moved.

The letter lay in the middle of the table.

Sam planted his elbows on the table, settled his face into his hands, closed his eyes, and gave out a loud sigh.

Chapter Four

NEW TEACHER

Michiko sat outside the drugstore on the wooden walkway, hugging her legs. She waited for the school security truck. Whenever Mr. Sagara drove it, Kiko got an early ride to school.

Before long, she saw it turn the bend and stop in front of the church. The little students got out. Kindergarten was in the church basement.

The truck drove down the street toward her and stopped. Kiko hopped out. She wore what most of the girls in the orchard wore to school. A light beige cardigan covered her pink-and-white-striped cotton blouse tucked into navy slacks. Michiko wore a green corduroy skirt to school today. Matching barrettes held her short, straight black hair behind her ears.

"I wonder what she looks like," Kiko whispered as they walked beneath the tattered awning of the Hardware Store School. The building sounded as hollow as a drum as they made their way to their partitioned classroom.

Michiko put her notebook on her desk. In the excitement of their letter, she had forgotten all about getting a new teacher.

Kiko lifted the wooden top of her desk and placed a small *furoshiki* inside. Michiko didn't have to bring a lunch to school. Her lunch waited for her across the street. On Fridays she brought Kiko home. Kiko eagerly looked forward to steaming *miso* soup and *tamago yaki*, made with Mrs. Morrison's farm-fresh eggs.

"I hoped we would meet her before anyone else," Kiko whispered.

Michiko looked at the blackboard. There was no date. The bottles of ink were still in a line along the window ledge. The stack of textbooks was missing from the teacher's desk.

"Are you sure there is school today?" she asked. But before Kiko could reply the clanging of the big brass bell brought the rest of the children running and pushing into the room.

In the bedlam of voices shouting and talking, Michiko covered her ears and sat down.

"Good morning, class," said a strong voice from behind them. A tall man with a big smile pushed aside the grey government blanket that acted as their class-room door. He strode to the front of the room and perched on top of the teacher's desk, waiting for the bedlam to subside.

"It's a man teacher," Kiko hissed behind her hand.

Michiko rolled her eyes. She could see that as plainly as the others. She put her face on her fists to listen, as the class sized up the bronze-skinned man with short black hair and chocolate eyes. He wore a knitted blue vest over a long-sleeved blue plaid shirt. A soft brown shoe with a single lace dangled from beneath the cuff of grey trousers.

"My name is Kaz Katsumoto," he said.

The boys in the room all began to talk at once.

"But you can call me," he said as he looked directly at the boys, "Mr. Katsumoto." He reached into his pocket and took out a small piece of chalk. Then he turned and wrote his name on the board. Several of the boys continued to murmur in excitement.

"Good morning, class," he said for a second time, when he finished writing.

"Good morning, Mr. Katsumoto," came the murmured reply.

"Is that the best you can do?" Mr. Katsumoto said in mock surprise. "I heard more noise that that walking into the room."

The boys at the back grinned. "Good morning, Mr. Katsumoto!" they yelled.

"Not bad," he responded, "but not good enough to cheer on a baseball team. Try again."

Michiko and Kiko looked at each other in surprise. This was the first teacher that asked them to be loud. Most expected them to be quiet.

"Good morning, class," he said to them for a third time and cupped his ear.

"Good morning, Mr. Katsumoto!" the entire class thundered.

"The first task of the day," Mr. Katsumoto began, "will be to determine our timetable." He opened the drawer of the desk and removed a small stack of paper. "But first I need to know your names." He walked to the back of the room and handed some paper to each person at the end of the row. As they passed the paper forward, Mr. Katsumoto said, "Match the paper perfectly corner to corner and then fold. Write your name below the fold and place it in front of you."

He waited as the children did as told. Then he walked up and down each of the rows reading each card out loud. He stopped at Kiko. She had not only folded the paper in half, she made a small fold on the front, creating a trough for her pencil "You like *origami*, Kiko?" Mr. Katsumoto asked.

Kiko blushed and nodded.

"Me too," he said. Then he asked the entire class, "Is anyone missing from class today?"

A girl at the front put up her hand. "Tamiko is not here," she informed the teacher. "Her mother had a baby last night and she won't be in school for a few days."

Mr. Katsumoto nodded in understanding. "Please make a card for her," he directed Kiko, handing her a piece of paper. "Even though she is absent, she is still part of our class."

Michiko liked the way this new teacher thought. When the tall, gawky girl named Tamiko returned, she would be pleased.

The new teacher stood in front of the blackboard, tossing the piece of chalk up and down in his hand. "Now," he announced, "we will create our timetable." He looked at them all and asked, "What do you want to learn?"

This question took everyone by surprise.

Kiko's hand shot up. "Our subjects should be English, mathematics, and social studies," she informed him with confidence.

He wrote the list on the blackboard then stood back and waited.

"I hope we can have art lessons," Michiko volunteered.

The teacher added them to the list. "Is there anything else?"

No one else spoke.

"There is one thing missing," Mr. Katsumoto remarked looking up and down the list. "We need the one subject necessary to one's mental alertness that takes a lot of daily practice."

The whole class groaned. What could this awful subject be?

He put the chalk to the board and paused. "I expect each and every one of my students to excel in this subject." He wrote the letters B-A-S-E, then paused and wrote B-A-L-L.

A cheer went up from the class.

"This way," Mr. Katsumoto informed them, pulling a familiar white ball from his pocket. "We will learn to be a team." He tossed the ball from hand to hand. "And we will save all our noise, energy, and excitement for the field. Is that understood?"

It was as if the new teacher had waved an invisible wand. All the students sat straight up, folded their hands on top of their desks, and looked straight ahead.

"How many of you are bilingual?" Mr. Katsumoto asked.

Kiko put up her hand. "I speak both English and Japanese."

Understanding what the strange word meant, several other children put up their hands. Michiko did not put hers up. She understood fragments of her grandfather's language, but she couldn't speak it with confidence.

"You know," Mr. Katsumoto said with a frown, "Japanese is not to be used at school."

~ ~ ~

"Mr. Katsumoto," Michiko told everyone at dinner, "says baseball teaches teamwork."

"Mr. Katsumoto?" her father said in surprise. "His first name couldn't be Kaz?"

Michiko nodded, her mouth too full of rice to speak.

"Did you hear that, Geechan?" Sam exclaimed. "Kaz Katsumoto is here!"

Geechan put down his chopsticks. "*Asahi* Katsumoto?" He put his dry spotted hands together and extended his arms, he swung them back then forward, then he cupped his eyes with his hand and followed an imaginary home run.

Chapter Five

SOYA SAUCE

After a day of sewing, helping with customers, and managing Hiro, Michiko's mother flopped into the wicker chair. A present from Mrs. Morrison, it groaned whenever anyone sat. Her mother's face was lined and her eyes puffy.

"Do you want me to make dinner?" asked Michiko.

Her mother nodded with gratitude.

Michiko measured the rice carefully. She washed it in a big bowl of water, rubbing the grains gently. She drained it and repeated. When the water ran clear she put it on to boil. That much she knew how to do. But they couldn't just eat rice. She opened the door and stared at the single lump of brown waxy paper in the icebox. Rice and bacon would have to do.

"Yoo-hoo," a woman's voice called out from the bottom of the staircase.

Michiko ran to open the apartment door for Mrs. Morrison. A yellow straw hat brimming with daisies sat askew on her cloud of carrot-coloured curls. The woman looked up and smiled. Her cheeks were pink from exertion. Behind her gold-rimmed spectacles, small blue eyes peeked out of a fleshy face. She put her dimpled hand on the frame of the door when she reached it. Her bosom heaved. The effort to get up the stairs took all of her breath.

"Is your mother here?" she asked blinking behind her spectacles. "If not I'll have to wait for her. I can't do those stairs more than once a day," she puffed.

"I'm here," Michiko's mother said rising from the chair. "This is a nice surprise."

Mrs. Morrison raised her string bag in salute. Michiko's mother took her by the arm and walked her to the kitchen. Edna placed the bag on the kitchen table — she never came to their house empty-handed. A jar of homemade pickles or jam, a cooking utensil, eggs; she brought anything that helped make their life easier.

"I'm making dinner," Michiko told her proudly. "I've already washed the rice and I'm going to chop up some bacon."

"Good thing I brought a cabbage," Mrs. Morrison replied, "and an onion."

"And add a touch of *shoyu*," her mother said. "Not much, be careful."

The shortage of soya sauce was becoming a problem for everyone who ate Japanese food. *Miso*, the special bean paste that most people used every day, was also in great demand. Her father had hung a hand-printed card reading THIS IS NOT A GROSHERY STORE in the drugstore window to stop people from asking.

Michiko filled the kettle and put it on the stove. The smell of frying onion filled the kitchen.

"I just left the church meeting," Edna began, reaching for the sugar bowl. It was one of her mother's china cups that had lost its handle. "While I was in town I thought I would visit." She rummaged about in her purse. "I need to take advantage of your sewing talents."

"A new dress?" her mother asked.

"Curtains," Edna replied. She opened her purse and pulled out a small brown paper bag. "One for each of us, and two for my little Heero," Edna said, referring to the oatmeal cookies.

Michiko smiled. Mrs. Morrison always pronounced her little brother's name incorrectly. She just couldn't get the inflection. She handed one to Hiro. He took it, examined it, then broke off a chunk and stuffed it into his mouth.

Mrs. Morrison explained the troubles she had getting the right material for new curtains. "I asked for poppy-coloured material, but they sent me scarlet, then wine, then purple." She took a sip of tea. "By the way, the church is thinking of having a bazaar."

"What's a bazaar?" Michiko asked. For some reason tents and elephants came to mind.

"It's like a fair," Edna said. "The town hasn't had one in some time," she told them.

"Why do people have them?" Michiko wanted to know.

"To raise money," Mrs. Morrison replied. "I'm sure the children in your school could do with some more books."

"The children need electricity first," Michiko's mother said. She picked up the teapot and filled her guest's cup. "Even if they had books, they would have to read them by oil lamp. Their eyes will be ruined if the electricity isn't installed."

"Perhaps I'll write the Red Cross," Edna suggested, sipping her tea.

Michiko thought about Kiko's news. How would they build a bathhouse if there wasn't any electricity? How would they heat the giant tub?

"Excuse me," she said. "I'll see if Geechan wants some tea."

"Tell him there is a cookie," Mrs. Morrison called out behind her.

Geechan squatted in the garden wearing a white handkerchief headband, pulling weeds. Dirt caked his big black rubber boots.

"Geechan," Michiko said to him, "Mrs. Morrison has a treat for you."

Her grandfather stood up and brushed the dirt from his hands. A huge grin crept across her grandfather's chestnut face.

"I have a question," Michiko said. She kicked a clump of earth with the toe of her shoe. The upturned earth smelled fresh. "How much water does it take to fill up an *ofuro*?"

Her grandfather scratched his head. Not always ready with an English reply, he made a large circular motion with his arms to explain.

"It's a lot, isn't it?" she said.

He nodded again and again.

"I have another question," she said.

He undid the bandana from the back of his head and used it to wipe his brow. Then he put it in his back pocket and waited for her to speak.

"Why would they build an *ofuro* where there's no electricity?"

He shrugged his shoulders and went into the house.

Michiko followed him inside. She went into the drugstore to see if her father had time for tea, but stopped when
she saw him reach for the bottle of chocolate syrup. *He's
making a milkshake*, she thought as he poured it into the
metal container. He added three large spoonfuls of malt
powder, and a glub of milk. As he fixed the container to the
mixer, a boy stepped out from behind the magazine rack.

Michiko caught her breath at the sight of the familiar
fringed cowboy vest and slingshot sticking out of the back
pocket. George King was the first person she met when
she walked to town. He almost ran her down with his
bicycle. George King called her a dirty Jap.

Michiko turned to leave just as he looked up and
spotted her.

"Hello," he said with a fake cowboy drawl, "fancy
meeting you here."

Michiko faced his cold hard gaze with a smile. "Hello,
George," she said politely. George had a loud voice and
used it anytime someone did not agree with him. The
moment he raised his voice, most people gave in, except
Michiko. She always spoke to him in a pleasant tone,
which infuriated him.

George took a dollar from his pocket and slapped it
on the counter. Her father put out his hand to take it, but
George pressed his finger to the edge of the bill. "Don't
even think of trying to rob me," he said. There was no
mistaking the scorn flashing from his cold blue eyes.

Michiko's father didn't answer. He returned with the
change, and placed it coin by coin in front of the boy.
"Have a good day," he said and went to the other side of
the store.

The pasty-faced boy finished his shake in long noisy slurps and belched. Then he left his stool and walked to the door. He squinted at the little hand-printed sign hanging from the doorknob and yanked it off. "Nobody wants this stupid English in their face," he told Michiko. "Your kind doesn't belong here, you know," he said, tossing the small square of cardboard onto the floor. He yanked the door open. "My dad's going to see to that."

Chapter Six

THE BATTHOUSE

The Nelson farm lay three miles off the main road, just outside town. This was where Michiko and her family had lived when they first arrived. Since there was an indoor pump and electricity, the Japanese community built their *ofuro* there.

Saturday afternoon, as the heat bugs zinged, Michiko waited at end of the road that led to the houses in the orchard. Her mother and Aunt Sadie had gone ahead carrying a small enamel basin, washcloth, and towels.

Michiko watched Kiko stop to say hello to the group of girls getting off a truck. They all wore khaki overalls with floppy straw hats tied under their chins. Some of them covered their arms with old nylon stockings. They giggled and talked, glad to finish their morning of berry picking.

Michiko was glad she didn't have to do that again. Once she went with Clarence. The dense stubby bushes were high in the mountains. The twigs and thorns scratched their legs. Because huckleberries ripened at different times, they had to pick them one-by-one. Michiko remembered scratched fingers, harsh sun, and mosquitoes.

That was before her father came home and got a job making thirty-five cents an hour. The apartment above the drugstore was free. According to Kiko's neighbour, Mr. Yama, Michiko's family was *kanemochi*, upper class.

Kiko finally broke away from the group and ran across the road. Swiping her hair from her face, she asked, "Is this your first time for *ofuro*?"

Michiko nodded. "We had nothing like it in our old neighbourhood." She didn't mention they were the only Japanese family on the street where she used to live.

They took the pine-scented path beneath the gigantic Douglas firs. Along the creek they watched dragonflies dart about the surface of the water. The ribbon of sunlight gleaming through the brush showed them the way out. Smoke wisped from the great black stovepipe sticking out of the roof of the slanted shed. Every time she saw the farmhouse she was grateful she no longer had to fetch a load of firewood or use the outhouse, especially in the winter.

Inside, Sadie was already soaking in the big square tub of sweet-smelling pine. The blue towel wrapped around her wet hair gave her skin the look of porcelain.

Her mother waited for them on the slatted wood floor. "All your clothes go on the bench," she instructed them. "Fold them neatly."

Michiko, embarrassed, exploded into a fit of giggles. "You first," she said to Kiko.

Kiko ripped off her clothes and threw them on the bench. She plopped onto a little four-legged stool. Michiko's mother dipped the bowl into the tub and drew out some hot water. She poured it over Kiko's naked body.

"Ahh," Kiko exclaimed. She turned to Michiko and smiled.

Michiko removed her socks and balled them up.

Eiko soaped the damp, steaming facecloth and then rolled it into a tight ball. Kiko squirmed and squealed as Michiko's mother scrubbed her vigorously from top to bottom.

"I cannot believe how dirty you are," Eiko said. She drew more water, rinsed, and washed again. Then Eiko handed the cloth to Kiko. "Each finger and each toe," Eiko told her. "You must learn to clean yourself thoroughly."

She took the cloth from Kiko and dropped it into the enamel basin at her side. "The cloth, once soaped, must never enter the bath," she instructed them both. Then she dipped the small wooden bucket into the big bath and dumped it over Kiko's back.

"Ahh," Kiko murmured with a sigh.

"Now you can climb into the tub," Eiko told her. She waved Michiko to the stool and bent to pick up the slushy, soapy cloth.

As soon as Michiko entered the hot water she felt like drifting into sleep. Opening one eye, she watched her mother cock her head to one side and squeeze out the water from her long dark hair. She used long pulling strokes like she was milking a cow. The water ran down her arm and dripped off her elbow.

"Is this only for Japanese people?" Michiko asked her.

"Why do you ask that?"

"I think Clarence should come," Michiko said. "I don't know how he uses a tiny tub."

"As long as he comes on men's day," Sadie said, "I'm sure it would be fine.

Michiko and Kiko exploded into a fit of giggles for the second time.

Kiko floated quietly. "Do you think my mother will ever get to come here?" Kiko asked. She sighed so deeply it made Michiko's heart ache.

Michiko's mother and her aunt exchanged an anxious glance.

"Where did your mother go?" Sadie asked. Michiko had always wondered what happened to Kiko's mother but was afraid to ask.

"She went to Japan, just before we had to move," Kiko said. "My father and my aunt sent letters to tell her where we are. But Mr. Yama says she will never come back."

Sadie gazed at the little girl across from her in a kindly way. "I don't think anyone has the power to tell the future," she said.

Michiko waited for her mother to say something, but all she said was *"Gangara."* That meant Kiko was to be patient.

"Mr. Yama says he has no desire to be part of this country," Kiko continued. "He says he wants to return to Japan because there is no future for any of us."

"I can see why he would say that," Sadie commented, flicking water at Michiko.

"I think that depends on what you want for a future," Eiko said.

"If you planned on travelling into the wild and being a prospector," Sadie said, splashing Michiko, "then this life would be fine for you."

Michiko giggled, returning her aunt's splash.

The wooden door of the shed opened abruptly as several girls arrived. "I have to go," they overheard one of them say. "There's a speaker coming from Toronto. I need to explain it all to my parents."

"Are you going to the meeting?" Kiko asked Michiko's mother as they dressed.

"My husband and father will be attending," Eiko responded. "I will be home with Hiro."

"Are you going to the meeting, Auntie Sadie?" Michiko asked, pulling up her socks.

Sadie held a small black oval-shaped mirror up to her face as she applied her lipstick. "Of course, all of the teachers want to hear what it is about."

"Why don't you come back to the orchard with me?" asked Kiko. "You can go home with your father."

They both looked at Michiko's mother in anticipation. She nodded in agreement.

Michiko and Kiko ran down the rutted dirt road, hand in hand.

"Ara!" Kiko yelled as she danced into the field. "Watch out for cow pies."

"What's a cow pie?" Michiko asked.

"You know, it's what cows leave behind in the field." She pointed to the numerous cow droppings that dotted the field like large brown pancakes.

Several cows stood in the shade of the apple trees. Their dark tails swished back and forth, disturbing the flies trying to settle. The two girls skipped their way across the field. Kiko made Michiko laugh, telling her how the orchard ladies scared the cows away by opening and closing umbrellas in their big black and white faces.

Stooping to pick buttercups and Queen Anne's lace, they heard the crack of a baseball bat and saw a ball soar skyward.

"Someone's playing baseball," Kiko yelled as they ran the rest of the way.

The girls watched the man in a red-and-white baseball cap jammed low across his forehead. He kept two, sometimes three, balls in the air at a time. He drove them easily to right field, then centre, then left. Racing after the balls, the boys from the orchard skidded and slipped in the dirt.

"It looks like Mr. Katsumoto," Michiko exclaimed. "I didn't know he lived in the orchard. I thought he lived up at the Bachelor House."

"He just moved in," Kiko replied. "Mr. Yama asked him to join his family so they could get a bigger house."

"That's good thinking," Michiko said.

"That's great thinking," Kiko replied. "Mr. Yama and his family will live at the other end of the orchard. I won't have to listen to him talk about my mother."

Michiko looked at her friend's face. She knew how much she missed her father when he was away. She couldn't imagine not having her mother with her. "You know what?" she said. "I think you are the bravest girl in the world."

Kiko studied Michiko's face before she replied. "I think you are brave too," she said. "I don't have *hakujin* friends."

Chapter Seven

THE MEETING

Everyone crowded into the long tarpaper building used as the meeting hall. Some people stood with their arms folded, spitting out Japanese fast and loud. Others talked in English about what had once been theirs, bristling with suspicion and anger.

Kiko and Michiko darted in and around them, listening to bits of conversation. The plank walkway was wide enough for two, but if you didn't watch where you were going your foot could slip off into the mud.

Kaz Katsumoto was also big news.

"I was only nine when I lived near Athletic Park," Kaz told the crowd of men that surrounded him. "I started off as a bat boy. I guess the rest is history."

"You were the youngest to join the *Asahi*," one of the men said. "I saw you play for the first time." He turned to tell the rest of the crowd, "As soon as the baseball left the pitcher's hand, Katsumoto was running from third to home plate."

None of the kids in Michiko's class planned to listen to what the visiting reverend had to say. They all wanted to investigate the fort one of the boys had built in an apple tree. Kiko couldn't; she had to stay close by just in case her father needed something from the house.

Michiko remained at her side. She hadn't yet located her father or grandfather.

The security truck rumbled down the rutted road and stopped. Michiko recognized Sadie among the group of teachers that got out. She put her two beautiful manicured hands to her chest and breathed in deeply. "I miss the smell of all that grass," she said to Michiko.

"I don't miss the wolves," Michiko said in response. She would never forget the night the hungry animals left the mountains and came right up to the farmhouse porch.

As Sadie and Michiko walked through the crowd they heard a long low whistle. "Looks like there still are a few wolves around," Sadie whispered in her ear. Then she put her hand up to pat the twist of hair at the nape of her neck. She was dressed in a wide-banded pink-and-white-striped cotton skirt and a sleeveless white blouse. Her perfume filled Michiko's nose, reminding her of the wild pink roses that grew along the roadside.

"Come and look at this," Kiko said, grabbing her elbow. She pulled Michiko in the direction of a group of men and boys standing beside a long yellow car with white-rimmed tires. Michiko's father was among them. She wondered if he was thinking about his black Ford with the long square snout.

Mr. Hayashi took the elbow of a man in the navy raincoat and fedora. He led him toward the building. The rest followed. Her father winked at them as he passed.

Kiko and Michiko walked around the car. It had a long narrow step under each door. The top half of the car's headlights were painted black, just like her father's had been. But the most amazing thing about it was the car had no roof.

"It's called a convertible," Kiko said. "I've heard about them but I've never seen one."

"Where is the roof?" Michiko wanted to know.

"It folds up," Kiko said, "like a baby carriage. When I grow up, I'm having one like it."

"We used to have a car," Michiko murmured. "We used to go for all kinds of rides."

But Kiko wasn't listening. She opened the door and jumped in behind the wheel. Kiko patted the seat beside her. "Get in, Michiko," she said. "We can go on holiday now."

Michiko put her hand on the chrome door handle, but hesitated. The reverend hadn't invited them to sit in his car. She turned to Mr. Katsumoto to see if he approved, but he was busy staring at someone in the crowd. Michiko followed his gaze to Sadie, in her white sleeveless blouse and crisp skirt, standing in the sunset.

"Get in, Michiko," Kiko repeated.

Michiko looked around. She pressed the large square button on the handle and pulled. The heavy yellow door swung open and Michiko climbed inside.

"You and I are going to drive to Toronto," Kiko announced turning the wheel.

"Why Toronto?" Michiko asked. "Let's go to Vancouver."

Kiko stopped moving the wheel and placed her hands down flat at her sides. "No one is ever going to Ban City," she said.

"Ban City," Michiko repeated. "Where's that?"

"You don't know anything, do you?" Kiko said with a great sigh. "I guess it's because you don't live in the orchard." She put her hands on her hips. "Ban City is Vancouver."

"Why?"

"Are you stupid?" Kiko asked with a smirk.

Michiko's mouth dropped open. No one had ever called her that. She put her hand on the door handle. "It's not nice to say that," she said.

Kiko grabbed her other hand in apology. "All Japanese people have been banned from Vancouver," she explained. "That's why it's called Ban City."

"But it's only for a while," Michiko murmured. "We will all be going back soon."

"Are you …" Kiko began, but stopped when Michiko glared at her. "Don't you know what the meeting is about?"

"No," replied Michiko in anger. She hated the way her parents kept things from her. Kiko knew about everything because her father ran the newspaper.

"The reverend," Kiko said, getting out of the car, "came from a church in Toronto."

Michiko wanted desperately to pretend she didn't care, but she couldn't. She opened the door and got out. "Why is he here?" she asked. "Does their church want to have a bazaar?"

"No," Kiko said. She pulled Michiko down on to the edge of the wooden walkway that joined the buildings. "The reverend wants the Japanese people to join his church."

"That's an awful long way to go to church," Michiko mused.

"Well," Kiko said, "we will all have to go somewhere."

Just then the wooden door opened and the crowd began to disperse. Most of them were speaking Japanese, which made it difficult for Michiko to understand. Whatever it was that they were discussing, it seemed important. Many walked with arms linked, deep in conversation. The crowd moved slowly toward their homes, replacing the sounds of the crickets.

"You won't have to walk back," Sadie announced as she left the building. "The truck was only half full. You can hitch a ride with us." She took Michiko's hand, beckoned to Sam, and pointed to the truck.

"Did you find it interesting?" asked Michiko.

"I'm not sure that is the correct word," Sadie responded.

Michiko looked up at her aunt. Usually Sadie insisted Michiko know all about what was going on with their lives. When Michiko's mother tried to cover the truth of their move, Sadie made sure Michiko understood it wasn't just a holiday. *Why was she being so secretive now?*

Her father sat in the back of the truck with his head resting on the canvas side with his eyes closed. She knew what his answer would be if she asked him.

"Adult business," he would say. "You stick to kid business."

Chapter Eight

HOME RUN

Mr. Katsumoto took the class to the vacant lot for their first baseball lesson. He pulled a white cap from his back pocket and shoved it down on his head. A large white *A* was embroidered above the bright-red brim. One of the boys whispered, *"Asahi,"* and they all grinned.

Baseball was all they talked about.

Michiko had never even held a bat.

At first they stood in a circle and Mr. Katsumoto tossed the ball to each of them in turn. "Easy does it," he coached them. "Just toss it back." He threw the ball with a round, smooth motion. It reminded Michiko of the way her Uncle Ted cast his fishing rod, only upside down.

When the ball came Michiko's way, she almost closed her eyes. But she caught it with both hands and smiled. The ball was a lot harder and heavier than it looked.

Mr. Katsumoto picked up the bat. "I'm going to teach you a game called Seven Up," he explained. "For every ball you catch in the air, you get three points. If it hits the ground and bounces, you get two points. If you pick it up from the ground you get one point."

The boys scrambled for position. Michiko realized this must have been what they were playing in the orchard.

Jennifer Maruno   49

He tossed the ball in the air and hit it toward them. "First one to get seven points becomes the next batter."

It didn't take long for Raymond to become batter. He caught two fly balls and a bouncer. He strutted up to the bat and clutched it with pride.

Michiko watched Kiko dart about the field, determined to be just as good. But when she shoved one of her classmates out of the way to catch the ball, Mr. Katsumoto whistled and shook his finger at her.

A louder whistle sounded in the distance. The train rumbled along the mountain, its massive headlight gleamed in the late afternoon sun.

"There's our signal to stop," Mr. Katsumoto called out. "School's out for the day."

The boys and girls raced back to the Hardware Store School to retrieve their belongings.

"Can't we play a little while longer?" Michiko asked. "Kiko is going to wait for the truck and I only have to walk down the street."

"Sure," Mr. Katsumoto replied. "I'll pick up my equipment on my way out."

"You hit," Michiko told Kiko, handing her the bat.

Kiko propped the bat over her shoulder. Michiko tossed the ball across the plate. Kiko swung before the ball arrived, lost her balance, and staggered. The ball dropped behind her. She turned and picked up the ball. "It's too hard with only two people," she complained.

"There's Clarence," Michiko said seeing him walk up from the tracks. "He can play with us." She waved him over.

"What a nice day," Clarence said sauntering toward them. "We should be fishing."

It was true. On such a glorious July day everyone should be fishing. But the Japanese children had missed one whole year of school and they had to make it up.

"We need another person," Michiko told him.

"Want to go fishing tomorrow?" Clarence asked.

Fishing when they should be in school? As pleasant as it sounded, it meant skipping. Michiko couldn't imagine doing anything that reckless. "Wouldn't Mr. Katsumoto get mad?"

"We could be sick for the day," Kiko said, clearly in favour of the idea.

"We couldn't bring our fishing rods to school." Michiko protested.

"I got a couple stashed for a day just like this," Clarence said. "Think about it."

Michiko tossed the ball again. This time Kiko hit it. The ball hit the ground at Clarence's feet and rolled though the grass. Clarence picked it up.

"Come on, Clarence," Michiko said, "play with us." She handed him the bat just as the security truck pulled up in front of the General Store.

Michiko sent a slow easy ball across the plate.

Clarence swung hard at the ball floating toward him, but nothing happened.

"Stee-rike one," Mr. Hayashi called out. He had come out of the Mounted Police Station just in time to see it. "You gotta keep your eye on the ball."

Clarence grinned. He beckoned Michiko to toss him the ball again and took the stance of a hitter. The ball came slow and low. Clarence swung hard. There was a loud crack. The ball ricocheted off the corner post of the station, landed on the roof of the truck, and bounced into the road.

Mr. Hayashi jumped into the road and retrieved it.

"Nice," Mr. Katsumoto called as he walked toward them. "We'll have to sign you up."

Mr. Hayashi tossed the ball to Mr. Katsumoto. Michiko and Kiko watched in anticipation as their teacher moved to the pitcher's mound. He stepped back, swung his arm as he took a step forward, and the ball left his hand. He threw hard and flat.

Clarence swung and the bat cracked for a second time.

The ball whistled past Michiko's ear and rose straight out over the road.

Clarence looked at the bat in surprise. "Holy mackerel," he murmured.

Everyone watched the ball disappear into the clouds before it sank into the lake.

"That one's gone for good," Mr. Katsumoto said, shielding his eyes with his hands.

"I'm really sorry," Clarence murmured. "I'll get you a new ball."

Mr. Katsumoto looked at him and laughed. "Not until you run the bases," he told him. "If you don't do that, you're out."

Clarence dropped the bat and ran around the thin, worn line that connected the four patches of dirt. As he headed for home he looked up and grinned.

Michiko jumped up and down clapping her hands. Mr. Hayashi pounded the side of his truck door. Mr. Katsumoto walked over and offered Clarence his hand.

"You must play a lot," he said to him with a grin.

"Nope," Clarence replied. "I think it was beginner's luck."

"Well, if you are a beginner," the baseball player said as he clapped his hand on Clarence's shoulder, "I expect to see you here practising with the rest of us."

"Would you?" Michiko asked.

Kiko pushed herself in between them. "He's not Japanese," she said in a peculiar voice.

Michiko turned to her in surprise. "What does that matter?' she asked.

"It doesn't," Mr. Katsumoto said in a low voice. He turned to Kiko. "No *haiseki* in baseball," he said in a firm way. Kiko dropped her head, turned, and ran to the truck.

"What did he mean?" Clarence asked.

"Mr. Katsumoto just wants Kiko to be a good sport," Michiko said. It was something told to her as long as she could remember. She was never to do anything to make trouble. Troublemakers shame a family.

That night Michiko told her father about playing baseball after school. "You should see Clarence hit," she bragged, "even Mr. Hayashi was surprised."

"You remember that squeeze play when the Asahi won the Terminal Championship?" her father asked Geechan. He took Geechan's chopsticks along with his and made a diamond shape on the table. The salt and pepper shakers became pitcher and batter.

"Here we go again," her mother said with a smile, "another moment in baseball history."

Geechan looked at Michiko. "Your father could have been Asahi," he told her. "They scout him."

"You could have played baseball?" Michiko repeated in surprise. "Why didn't you?"

"I was on the road," was her father's reply. "I needed the job for my family."

The next afternoon when Clarence joined them on the field, the man from the General Store brought a chair outside to watch. Mr. Hayashi drove the truck in early. Even the Mountie on duty stuck his head out the door once or twice.

When Sam showed up, Clarence handed him the bat. He smiled and rolled up his sleeves.

Kiko dropped to the sidelines. "The adults are taking over," she complained.

"I've got an idea," Michiko whispered. "Our class should challenge them."

"You mean like a real game?" Kiko asked in astonishment.

"You could even report on it for your father's newspaper," Mihiko suggested.

Mr. Katsumoto liked the idea a lot. He invited Mr. Sagara and Mr. Hayashi to be on the team. Michiko suggested her father and Uncle Ted.

"What will be the name of your team?" Mr. Katsumoto asked Kiko.

Kiko looked at Michiko and shrugged.

"I know," Michiko said. "We can be the Main Street Team."

"That makes us the Orchard Team," Mr. Katsumoto responded.

The class practised after school and chose their best players.

The adults practised after dinner.
Geechan coached them all.

Chapter Nine

THE GAME

Michiko's mother stuffed rice bags with newspaper for the bases. Ted erected a small wooden platform. On it he put three chairs and a small table. His carpentry business made all the chairs and tables for the people in the orchard.

The news had spread. Everyone was coming to watch the game.

Clarence and Michiko waited on the edge of the platform for the rest of the team to arrive. She noticed the little scars that marked his bare white knees. Close to him, Michiko could smell Clarence's body. He had a woody smell, like a fireplace. It was not a bad smell, but a definite one. She knew her grandfather smelled of fish and soap and her mother of warm sweet baking. She guessed every person had a smell and wondered what hers might be.

Somewhere a cicada buzzed. Clarence looked at the clear cloudless sky. "Perfect day for baseball," he said.

"Are you the boy who hit the ball into the lake?" a small Japanese man asked Clarence.

Clarence looked up in surprise and nodded.

"You can't play without a glove," the man said. He held out a baseball glove with fingers stitched and tied several times. "It's good and solid," he said, smacking the old leather mitt with his fist.

Clarence reached out to touch the smooth walnut brown leather.

"I polish it with oil once a week," the man told him. "It's old like me, but a classic." He handed Clarence the glove. "Can't play ball without a glove," he repeated, walking away to join the gathering crowd.

Clarence stared up at the man in disbelief. Then he put the glove to his face, closed his eyes, and drank in the smell of leather.

Fine clouds of dust rolled up behind the wheels of an old lumber truck. Several men jumped out and unloaded chairs for those who needed to sit.

Behind it came the Security Commission truck. Kiko waved from the front as the rest of their team emptied out of the back. Then it turned around.

"I bet he's going back for more people," Clarence said miserably.

"Of course," Michiko squealed, circling her arms in the air. "This is going to be big."

"I wonder if Mrs. Morrison is going to come," Clarence said. No sooner had he spoken than Bert's familiar green pickup truck rounded the corner.

"Yoo-hoo," their stout friend called out from the window, waving the tip of her knitted shawl. Mrs. Morrison's rocking chair bounced about the truck bed as Bert pulled on to the field.

Sadie, waving madly, pointed to the truck. Michiko watched her family join Mrs. Morrison in the back. Geechan stumbled getting up, but her mother caught his arm.

Bert ambled off to the crowd of townsfolk gathering nearby.

"Good luck," Michiko whispered to Clarence. Kiko beckoned, paper and pencil in hand.

As Michiko headed toward the truck, two boys from her school were walking beside her. She couldn't help overhearing their conversation.

"He can't just push us around like that," the small one complained.

The bigger boy got in front of him and took hold of him by the shoulder. "Listen," he said, giving the small boy a shake, "you should have just kept quiet."

"All I said was he never played baseball," the small boy grumbled.

"That George kid doesn't want to have anything to do with us," the bigger boy explained. "You should have walked away."

"All I said was the truth," the small boy protested in anger. "You can tell by the way he threw the ball into the bushes he'd never played baseball. What's wrong with telling the truth?"

"That's why he shoved you in the dirt. You can't make fun of *hakujin.*"

"George …" Michiko repeated. "Excuse me," she said, turning to the boys, "was it George King? Was he the boy you had a problem with?"

"All I know is his first name is George," the bigger boy said. "He hates Japanese."

"He knocked me down when I tried to get my ball back," the little boy complained. "He said it was his ball, because it was on his property and his family owned the whole town."

"I tried to make him give it back," his older brother said. "He shoved me too."

Michiko nodded in sympathy as a roar went up from the crowd. Kaz Katsumoto had mounted the platform. The boys and Michiko rushed to watch the game.

Mr. Hayashi picked up the megaphone and welcomed the crowd. Mr. Katsumoto and Raymond, their team captain, flipped a coin. Everyone took their places. As she settled herself in the back of the truck, Michiko refused to think about George anymore.

"Stepping up to the plate is Kobe Arai," the announcer called out. "Pitching for the adult team is Kaz Katsumoto, known to many as the 'Man with the Golden Arm.'"

"I didn't know that," Kiko exclaimed, writing rapidly. Then she put the end of the pencil in her mouth and chewed it nervously as she watched.

Kaz Katsumoto rolled the ball in his fingers. Then he readied himself, reared back, and fired the ball toward the plate. *SAAAWAAK* was all they heard. The ball hit the catcher's glove right in the centre of the pocket.

"Stee-rike one," the umpire called out.

"Here comes the pitch," the announcer told the crowd. "Arai swings. Ladies and gentlemen, kiss it goodbye."

The crowd whooped, whistled, and clapped as Kobe ran home.

"First ball to find its way into the lake," the announcer commented.

"The second ball into the lake," Michiko said smugly. "Clarence's was first."

"Clarence the Red is a hard hitter and a skilled outfielder," the announcer said.

Clarence shot a nervous look at the crowd.

"Clare-ence, Clare-ence," the kids from town shouted from the roof of the General Store.

"Hi, Clarence," Hiro's small voice called out. The crowd chuckled.

Clarence raised his eyes to the sky and then faced the pitcher.

Michiko glanced at Geechan. "He looks scared," she said. Her grandfather patted her shoulder, keeping his eyes on the boy.

From a full windup, Mr. Katsumoto shot one across the plate. Clarence watched it go past for a called strike.

The next pitch flew across his knees for strike two. The third pitch whizzed in like an arrow. It looked slightly high, but Clarence swung.

"You're out!" said the umpire.

A huge sigh came from the crowd.

Clarence slung his bat in despair.

Michiko watched him walk back to the bench, head bowed. "He feels bad," she said.

"What do you expect?" Kiko said. She bent her head and wrote with fury. "He's playing against *Asahi*!"

Michiko saw Raymond put his hand on Clarence's shoulder and speak. Clarence nodded, even though he seemed occupied with the webbing on his glove.

Raymond went to bat. He managed a pop fly but the fielder caught it.

"They're pulling down balls like bees to honey," Kiko commented in Japanese as she wrote. Geechan nodded and smiled.

The adults went up to bat.

"Here's a man that followed the dream of every young boy. He wore the Asahi uniform at the age of nine." The announcer introduced Kaz Katsumoto. "Katsumoto started out as a Clover, became a Beaver, worked his way through the Athletics, and is here today as Asahi."

Kiko wrote as quickly as she could.

Kaz Katsumoto went to bat. He smashed the first pitch deep to the left field where it ricocheted off the front of the General Store. The boys from the orchard, lining the field, yelled and cheered as Kaz Katsumoto made his way home.

Michiko watched the baseball streak toward her Uncle Ted. It dropped into the catcher's glove. "Stee-rike one," the umpire called out. The next pitch was faster. Ted didn't look at anyone else except the pitcher. The ball smacked into the catcher's glove.

"Stee-rike two," was the call.

On the third pitch Ted hit it up the middle. The pitcher dove but missed the ball. When he finally threw it to first the baseman caught it with a loud plop, but too late to tag the runner.

"Yay, Uncle Ted," Michiko called out. Everyone in the truck bed clapped.

"You are cheering for the wrong team," Kiko told her with a roll of her eyes.

The sun moved lower in the sky. No one paid much attention when Geechan stepped down from the truck. Hiro followed him and Michiko had to chase him down. "Stay here," she said when she handed him back to her mother.

"It's two down and Clarence the Red has two strikes," the announcer called out.

The crowd went quiet.

Clarence raised his chin and hunched his body, this time determined to give it his all.

The third pitch was like the first two.

Clarence bunted and raced for first, just as Geechan taught him. The catcher threw, but the baseman missed. Clarence headed for second. The ball rolled out to right field, where Mr. Hayashi fumbled it. Clarence made it to third.

Mr. Hayashi threw the ball home but the catcher was talking to someone.

"Head for home, head for home," the crowd chanted.

Clarence tripped on a lump in the field, fell and scrambled along the ground, and dove into home plate as the catcher picked up the ball.

Applause and laughter exploded from the fans.

"A home run all on errors?" yelled Kiko. She shook her head unbelievingly.

"That's Clarence," bragged Michiko, glancing at the group of farmers off to one side. They were cheering and clapping each other on the back. She saw Bert leave the group and approach Mr. Katsumoto.

The crowds broke up in the deepening dusk. "Who would have thought," Michiko heard one woman say, "we would be watching baseball again."

"With such handsome players," another commented.

"The men around town have been looking for something to do," Mrs. Morrison said, fanning herself with a piece of folded newspaper. "Maybe they can get a team together."

Michiko climbed down to tell Geechan the news. But as she rounded the front of the truck she gasped. Her grandfather lay face down in the dirt. Her scream brought her mother and Aunt Sadie to his side.

Bert, Ted, and Sam raced across the grass to see what was happening. Bert tossed Mrs. Morrison's rocking chair over the side and helped to lift Geechan into the back of truck. They covered him with Mrs. Morrison's shawl.

Michiko clutched Kiko's hand as the green truck raced its way to the hospital.

Chapter Ten

SPLASH

September brought the smell of dry leaves that always reminded Michiko of newly sharpened pencils. But the days of starting school with a new satchel full of coloured pencils and clean notebooks were long gone. Clarence and Michiko met at their usual spot on the bridge at the outskirts of town. Here the icy creek raced out of its forest tunnel and plunged over the rocks.

"How's Geechan?" he asked.

Michiko shrugged and smiled. It was hard to explain her grandfather's "far-offness." His eyes glazed over when they talked. Whenever he spoke he ran out of breath before he could finish what he had to say. His jaw fell open when he slept in the chair. Sometimes his hand just dropped to his side, spilling his tea. He seemed to have no more strength than a kitten.

The sun reflected off a brightly polished bicycle fender coming toward them. Michiko grimaced. The only good thing about seeing George was it reminded her how lucky she was to have Clarence for a friend.

"Where ya going?" he shouted, screeching his wheels and sending up a shower of stones.

"Where do you think?" Clarence replied. He held up

his fishing rod as a hint. The cork bobber swung back and forth from the string that dangled from a tree branch.

"You won't catch anything with that," mocked George. "I suppose your pretending to be Indians again." Once Clarence fooled George by telling him Michiko was a full-blooded Kootenay. George hadn't forgotten or forgiven.

"Buzz off," Clarence said as they turned up the lane that led to the orchard. They both knew George wouldn't follow them there.

Saturday was the day the men in the orchard left town to cut wood. They boarded the Security Commission truck under the supervision of Mr. Hayashi. Kiko passed her father his lunchbox. "At least they get to leave the orchard," she complained to Michiko.

"Why don't you come with us?" Michiko asked her friend.

"I don't have a rod," Kiko said.

"We can share mine," offered Michiko. "Just think: fresh fish for dinner.

Kiko grinned. She waved goodbye to the truck and the three of them headed past the last of the houses into the woods.

At the end of the street the three of them came face to face with Mr. Yama. The small wiry man crossed his arms *batsu* and stood in their way, glaring. The dark skin of his arms and face seemed shrivelled. His stale chocolate eyes sank deep into their red-rimmed sockets. Because of the large purple birthmark that marred half of his face, Michiko found it hard to look at him.

The man squinted as if he could not believe who stood in front of him. "Why you *hakujin* here?" he shouted. He pointed a bony finger at Clarence. "What you want?" he growled.

"Just ignore him," Kiko said.

"You and you," he said, brandishing his finger at Michiko and Clarence, "ENEMY."

"You can't say that," Michiko protested, seeing Clarence's face go slack.

"Mr. Yama," Kiko said, grabbing Michiko's fishing rod. She held it up. "Michiko and I are going fishing. Be nice to her."

"Bah," Mr. Yama spat out and moved aside.

"What a miserable old guy," Clarence said as they headed toward the lake. "He needs a drum to bang."

Kiko turned back and yelled, *"KI-CHIGAI GEECHA."*

Michiko shook her head. Calling Mr. Yama a crazy old man wouldn't help anything. Michiko's mother told them he had a lot of problems because of his face and had trouble letting go of his misery. But that wasn't the only thing that bothered Michiko about Kiko. She should have told Mr. Yama to be nice to Clarence as well.

They headed toward the beach. It wasn't really a beach but a rim of sand along the lake, beaten down by the number of people that used it. The lake sat still and calm. The reflection of the tall rugged mountains was as sharp and precise as the mountains themselves. It was so still it almost seemed wrong to break the silence by talking.

"Do we fish from here?" Kiko asked.

Michiko shook her head. She led them along the strip of firm, damp sand. Then they scrambled through the bushes, slipping on the small, round pebbles that lined the shore.

"Where are we going?" Kiko whined, slapping at a mosquito.

"Wait and see," said Clarence.

Kiko watched Clarence and Michiko part the branches of a fallen willow. The small red rowboat nodded under an archway of greenery.

"Wow," Kiko exclaimed. "You have a boat? Where did you get it?"

"My uncle made it," Michiko told her with pride. "We call it the *Apple*."

Clarence stepped on to the fallen tree trunk, walked along it, and tossed his fishing rod into the boat. Then he returned and took Michiko's rod. Michiko clutched Clarence's other hand as she climbed up and followed. Kiko scrambled up and along the trunk with ease. The branches swayed in the water when she got into the boat.

Soon they were gliding past shores of green grass. Kiko trailed her hand in the clear, cold mountain water. Michiko inhaled deeply. She loved the strong weedy smell of the lake. She could almost taste its ancientness.

"We have a special fishing spot," Michiko said. "But don't tell anyone, it's a secret."

"How did you find it?" Kiko asked.

"The Indians showed us the way," Clarence said, making Michiko laugh.

A speckled trout rose from the water with its mouth open and snapped at a fly. Kiko clapped her hands in delight. Clarence nudged the boat toward the bank where the creek began to bend. They spent the morning drifting about the small cove surrounded by steep banks. Three trout soon lay at Clarence's feet. Michiko caught several as well. Kiko didn't even try.

"Time to head back," Clarence said. "No need to be greedy."

The three of them looked up at the sound of snapping twigs. Michiko saw a flash of a green-and-white-checked shirt at the top of the bank. Then she heard a familiar voice. "Where did you get the boat, Clarence?"

The three of them searched the bushes with their eyes.

George's voice shouted out again. "Hope it's your boat, Clarence," he shouted. "It's against the law for Japs to own one."

"We know it's you, George," Clarence called back. "Scared to show your face?"

George came out from behind a large bush and stood at the edge with his hands on his hips. "I asked you a question, Peach Boy," George shouted. "Who owns the boat?"

Clarence and Michiko looked at each other wide-eyed.

"I do," Clarence shouted back.

Kiko looked at Clarence and then at Michiko. She stood up with eyes blazing. "You couldn't build a boat like this," she yelled. "This is Japanese-built. It's the best!"

Michiko looked at her in horror. Her uncle had painted the hull rough, so no one would suspect. Normally he took the time to strain the paint twice, making it glide on like silk.

"No, Kiko," she insisted as a wave of panic rose inside her. "Clarence built it." If the Security Commission found out Ted had a boat, he would be in trouble. They would think he was a spy for sure. "I watched him do it," Michiko shouted back.

"You're lying," George screamed. "You told me once boats were much better than bicycles. That uncle of yours built it, didn't he?"

"Let's get out of here," Michiko said, pulling Kiko down so hard she almost toppled over the side. They grabbed the oars and turned the boat around. But Kiko wasn't finished. She turned to George, stuck out her tongue, and then screamed in Japanese, *"BAKA, BAKA!"*

"I'll get you," George threatened as he took a step forward shaking his fist. But his weight on the edge of the grassy bank made it collapse. He slid down into the water.

"Ha, ha, ha," Kiko said as she laughed and pointed. "Look at the big fish swim."

But Michiko could tell by the way George was flaying about that he wasn't swimming.

"Clarence," she screamed, "I don't think George can swim."

George's face rose from the rippled waters of the cove sputtering. "Help," he wailed.

Michiko jumped into the water. The icy cold bit right through her clothes and took her breath away. Holding on to the side of the boat, she extended her other arm to the thrashing boy. "Take my hand," she called out to him, but she couldn't quite reach him.

Clarence handed Michiko an oar. "Grab the paddle, George," he yelled.

George clutched at the wide end of the oar with both hands. As Kiko and Clarence dragged the oar closer, Michiko grabbed the shoulder of his shirt and pulled him to the boat.

"Hang on," Michiko said, catching her breath, "until we reach the rocks."

Clarence drew the boat in. Michiko dragged George up onto a wide, warm rock. He slumped down shivering with cold and shaking with fear.

Michiko turned on Kiko. "Why did you have to say that?" she demanded. "If he tells the Mounted Police they will take the boat." She put her hands on her heart. "They could even take my uncle away."

"Okay," Kiko responded with a shrug. "Then we'll just dump him back in."

Michiko looked at Clarence in surprise.

"Don't," George yelled, crawling back in terror. "Clarence, you got to save me from these Japs."

Clarence's eyes narrowed. "Why should I?"

George sucked in his breath.

In a quiet voice, Michiko spoke to the soaking, scared boy. "You better keep this boat a secret if you don't want enemies for real." She waved her hand toward the exposed roots of the river bank. "You can climb back up over there."

George scrambled to the top of the bank. His face crumpled as he stood watching them row away. "It's not fair," he sobbed. "Clarence has all kinds of brothers and sisters." He wiped the water from his face. "I don't have any friends at all."

"Then you should remember this Japanese saying," Michiko called out to him. *"Always beware of the returning arrow."*

Chapter Eleven

THE TELEGRAM

The maple trees on Main Street made the papery rustle of autumn. It was a nice day for October, but it was way before suppertime and the sky was already getting dark. The wind prowled about Michiko and Kiko's feet like a cat, reminding them that winter was on its way. Each carried a large brown paper bundle up the road. Where they walked, green, spiked balls and shiny black nuts littered the woodsy yards.

"I hate walking home in the dark," Kiko whispered. "I wish I had a flashlight."

If I had a flashlight, Michiko thought, *I would read in bed*. But like everything else, it cost money. "It will be okay," Michiko reassured her, "Mrs. Morrison promised us a ride back."

They approached the large wooden house with scrolls of woodwork around the front verandah. Yellow leaves covered the woodsy lawn. In the summer you could hardly see the Morrison's house for honeysuckle and clematis. Now a cloud of dead branches and leaves, still attached to the lattice, rattled in the wind.

Michiko put down her bundle and pushed open the gate. They mounted the wide wooden steps and knocked. The door was partly open.

"That'll be the girls," Mrs. Morrison boomed out from the kitchen. She had such a large voice they could hear it on the verandah.

A tall woman in a long-sleeved black blouse, black skirt, stockings, and stout black shoes bustled toward them. Her skinny red nose looked as if it had been in a pencil sharpener. Seeing Michiko and Kiko the woman stopped suddenly, making the eye glasses on a chain around her neck bounce. "Are *you* the girls from town?" she asked in a sharp, vinegary voice. Her lips puckered in disapproval.

Michiko felt her face redden. *When you are at home or school, you forget about being Japanese*, she thought. *But when people look at you the way this woman does, you remember.*

"Give Mabel your coats," Edna boomed from the kitchen. "I'm up to my elbows."

Michiko placed her mittens and hat on the small table beside the door.

Kiko had come without.

Mabel shook each coat before hanging it up, as if she expected something to fall out.

"We're just kids," Michiko wanted to call out after her. *"We are not spies."* Instead she adjusted the blouse under her navy blue jumper. Her freshly ironed, long-sleeved white blouse had mother-of-pearl buttons that turned blue and pink in different lights.

Kiko paused in the doorway of the living room. She stared at the couch, Persian rug, pictures on the wall, and the heavy bronze lamp with the green fringed shade. Kiko placed her hand on the dark wood banister of the staircase that led to the second floor and glanced up. Michiko could tell by the look on her face that she wanted to explore.

The girls entered the kitchen to see Mrs. Morrison's pudgy fingers rolling out soft yellow pastry dough. She was a wide woman, and her white apron made her even wider.

"What kind of pie are you making?" Michiko asked.

Edna Morrison paused with the rolling pin in the centre of the flattened circle. "It wouldn't be a Thanksgiving without mincemeat pies," she bragged. "This is the last for today."

"What kind of meat do you put in?" Michiko asked.

"None," Mrs. Morrison said with a smile. "It's really just a fruit pie."

Kiko gave the dark mixture of raisins, apples, and pears in the earthenware bowl a stir. "So, there is no meat in a mincemeat pie." She repeated it as if to store the information.

Edna folded the circle of dough in half and slid it into the pie pan. "Why don't you two run downstairs and get a jar of jam from the shelf." She dipped her head in the direction of the door that led to the basement.

The two girls made their way down to the dank room of cinder-block walls and earthen floor. A single bare light bulb cast harsh shadows on the walls, a silver cobweb glistening from its enamel collar. A large shelf of filled jars sat between the wringer washer and the furnace.

Preserves of pallid pears, golden peaches, and crimson crabapples filled the top shelf. The bottom shelf was full bread and butter, mustard, and dill pickles. Michiko reached out to the middle shelf lined with jars of peach, strawberry, gooseberry, and black current jam.

"What kind do you want?' she asked.

Kiko shrugged. "I've only ever tasted strawberry," she confessed.

"Then try something new," Michiko suggested, reaching for a jar of golden yellow.

"It's such a big house," Kiko whispered to Michiko. "Does she live here all by herself?"

Michiko nodded. "This is where Mrs. Morrison grew up. After her parents died, she and her husband came here to live. But then he went off to war."

~ ~ ~

"Now tell me all about your plans for Christmas," Mrs. Morrison asked, heading for the kitchen sink with her arms in the air when the girls returned to the kitchen. "Is your class having a party?"

Michiko and Kiko glanced at each other. No one had said anything about a party. "Maybe we should suggest it," Michiko said to her friend.

"The school Christmas party was the highlight of the year when I was young," Mrs. Morrison reminisced. She gave the handle of the water tap a nudge with her elbow. "Oh!" she exclaimed. "Will one of you undo my watch?"

Kiko raced to Mrs. Morrison's assistance. She undid the clasp of the tiny gold strap, letting the watch fall into her hand. "It's so delicate," she said.

"Just an old thing," Mrs. Morrison said. "Put it on top of the mantel." Reaching for the sliver of yellow soap by the sink, she told Michiko to stick some slices of bread into the toaster. "Jam on toast always brightens up a dreary day," she said with a smile.

Michiko sliced two pieces of bread and clamped them into the wire rack on the burner.

"Who was the lady that answered the door?" Kiko asked returning to the kitchen.

Michiko frowned at her impertinence.

"That's Mabel, Bert's wife," Edna explained removing her apron. "She helps me with my dusting and cleaning."

"Why can't she help you hang your curtains?" Kiko asked.

Michiko rolled her eyes. How many times had her mother told her not to ask questions about other people's business? But then, Kiko didn't have a mother.

"Same reason we no longer pick our own apples," Mrs. Morrison replied, after a hearty laugh. "Neither of us can get up a ladder."

By the time the old curtains had come down and the new ones were up, it had gotten dark.

The feast of pork chops, peas, turnip, mashed potatoes, and gravy stuffed them beyond belief. Michiko gave a huge groan. Kiko rubbed her stomach and rolled her eyes.

Mrs. Morrison looked at her wrist to check the time. "I forgot, I took off my watch," she admitted. But no sooner than she had spoken the tall clock in the hall chimed seven.

"Get your coat girls," their hostess directed. "Your ride will be here any minute."

There was a knock on the door just as the girls picked up the bundles of old curtains. "That'll be Bert," Mrs. Morrison said. "He's driving you both home." She turned to each of the girls and gave them a warm hug.

But it wasn't Bert at the door.

A man in a brown uniform with khaki puttees topping his highly polished boots waited in the yellow porch light. Under his large peaked cap a pencil stuck out from behind his ear. He held out a flimsy yellow envelope with the words Western Union.

Mrs. Morrison stopped in the hallway and put her hands to her chest.

"Edna Morrison?" the man asked, looking past the girls.

Michiko and Kiko swerved their heads to see the woman in the foyer shake her head. She didn't put out her hand to take it.

Kiko snatched it from the man's hand. "I'll give it to her," she said.

The man looked down at her in surprise. Then he looked at Mrs. Morrison frozen in the doorway and tipped his hat. "Good night," he said and closed the door behind him.

"I knew it would happen. I've been right about everything that has to do with this war," she said in a dull voice. "Just when I finally stopped worrying," she whispered, "I get a telegram."

Michiko led the frightened woman to the living room and eased her on to the couch.

Kiko brought the envelope.

"But you don't know what it says," Michiko told her gently. "You have to open it."

"I know what it says," she murmured, taking the telegram. She turned it over and over.

"Stop talking," Kiko interrupted. "Open the telegram."

Michiko's head jerked up in surprise. But Kiko's rudeness seemed to get through to Mrs. Morrison. She tore open the envelope.

It seemed to take forever to remove the thin piece of paper with funny typing from its envelope. But Mrs. Morrison couldn't seem to read it. She just held it in front of her and stared.

"Read it," Michiko urged.

The two of them watched the pair of gold-spectacled blue eyes finally travel back and forth across the print. Then, with a sigh, Edna Morrison folded it and stuffed it back into the envelope. She held it to her chest and breathed in deeply.

"A torpedo hit his ship," she said.

Michiko and Kiko gasped and looked at each other with wide eyes.

"It sank," she continued.

The room was silent but for the tick of the clock.

"They are searching for survivors," she finally added. "Ralph Morrison is missing in action." Edna Morrison searched Michiko's face.

"I'm not even able to cry," she said in surprise.

There was a second knock on the front door. This time it was Bert, in his red plaid coat and denim overalls.

"Mr. Morrison's ship sank," Kiko blurted out as she yanked open the door.

"He's missing in action," Michiko added.

Bert removed his cap, rushed inside, and kneeled at Mrs. Morrison's side. "He'll be fine," he said. "Remember the time he lost his oars fishing? He knows how to keep afloat."

"I don't think we should go home," Michiko said, taking the woman's hand in hers. "Mrs. Morrison shouldn't be left alone at a time like this."

Bert looked at her in surprise. "I'll go get Mabel," he said.

Michiko tossed the bundle of old curtains into the back of the pickup truck and lifted her knee to crawl up on top. Bert removed the pipe from between his brown stained teeth and held it in his hand. "No need to ride in the back," he said. "There's room for the two of you up front."

No one spoke as they followed the glare of truck beams along the dark road. At the laneway to the orchard, the truck slowed down.

"Which place is yours?" he asked.

"Follow the road to 8th Street," Kiko told him. "I'm in the first house."

Kiko hopped out, stopped in front of the truck, and waved goodbye. The headlight caught something on her wrist, making a flash. Michiko wondered what it was.

Within minutes the green truck pulled up the back lane of the drugstore. Michiko paused with her hand on the handle. "That was nice of you to take Kiko right to her door," she said.

Bert nodded and then spoke. "How's your grandfather doing?"

Michiko smiled briefly. Her grandfather looked so tired and his memory was not quite right. He kept calling her Eiko and asked her all kinds of thing about people she never knew. "The doctor told him he'll be fine if he takes it easy and stops running around coaching baseball," she said.

For the first time, Michiko saw the tall, solemn farmer grin.

"Tell him from me," he said, "that's good news for the farmers' team. He's much too good a coach."

Michiko placed the first bundle of curtains inside the door at the foot of the stairs. When she went back for the second, she smiled. She had just realized her grandfather would like very much like to hear what Bert just said.

Chapter Twelve

THE DATE

"Eat something." Michiko heard her mother tell Sadie in the kitchen. "You shouldn't go anywhere on an empty stomach. It might rumble."

"When this war is over," Sadie said, "I'm going to eat cake every day."

Eiko laughed. "If you eat cake every day," she replied, "you will be fat, like me."

Michiko put down her book and smiled. Even if Sadie ate cake every night, she knew it would only be a very small piece. She was proud of her slim figure. Sadie wore dresses with belts so tight it was a wonder she could breathe. But her mother wasn't as slim as she used to be, which was strange because none of them were eating cake. Her mother seemed to have gotten thicker about the waist.

Michiko went into the kitchen. "Do you want me to bake a cake tonight?" she teased.

"I'm too nervous to eat anything," her aunt replied. Sadie picked an invisible piece of lint from her shoulder. "I've got a date," she murmured.

"A date?" Michiko and her mother repeated at the same time.

"Where did you meet him?" her mother wanted to know.

"Where else would I meet him?" Sadie responded with a laugh. "It's not as if we get to travel anywhere outside of this town."

Michiko was not surprised that Sadie had a date. She was so beautiful that the farmhouse could have been full of men wanting to take her out. But this was the first time since they left Vancouver she even used the word.

"Is he handsome?" Michiko asked.

"I don't know," Sadie said in a whisper.

"You don't know what he looks like?" Michiko asked in awe. "Why not?"

"It's a blind date," Sadie told them. Then she lowered her voice. "And neither of you are to say anything about this to Geechan."

Michiko glanced at the closed door of her grandfather's bedroom.

"Sadie," her mother began, but Sadie put up her hand to stop her.

"I'm not going to discuss it with him," she said. "I live outside the home, and I'm old enough to know what I am doing. You know how old-fashioned he is. He'll expect me to have a chaperon."

"Or at least a go-between," Eiko said with a smile.

"What's a go-between?" Michiko wanted to know.

"A go-between is a person who arranges for you to meet the man you will marry."

Michiko looked at her mother. Her flowered pinafore stretched across her front as if it had shrunk in the wash. "Did you have a go-between?"

"Yes," she said. "A go-between put your father and me together."

"I suggested the match," Sadie said. "Can you just imagine if they had picked someone like Mr. Yama?"

Michiko's mouth dropped. Sadie burst into laughter at the sight.

"Stop teasing, Sadie," Eiko said. "You'll have Michiko believing the strangest things."

"What are you going to wear?" Michiko asked. She loved it when her aunt used to visit them right after her day in the dress shop. She had so many beautiful outfits. Her shoes always matched her purse. Once she wore a veiled hat made completely of red feathers.

"I don't know," her aunt responded. For a moment she stared off into space. "I think I'll start out wearing grey. I don't want to waste a good outfit on someone who might be boring." She smoothed out her skirt as she talked. "I wish I had enough money to make a new dress." She lifted her tea cup to her lips, and then paused. "And what about you, Eiko?" she said. "What are you going to do about a new wardrobe?"

Eiko put one finger to her lips and gave Sadie a wide stare. "Mrs. Morrison has offered me a few of the dresses she no longer wears."

"Mrs. Morrison," shrieked Michiko. "Her dresses would be way too big for you."

"Your mother has a sewing machine, doesn't she?" Sadie responded.

~ ~ ~

Sadie wasn't coming for lunch the following Sunday because she had a second date with the-man-no-one-knew. They planned to spend the day in the mountains. Eiko was making them a picnic.

"Do you think Auntie Sadie will get married?" Michiko asked her mother as they wrapped rice balls in wax paper.

"In Japan, girls get married at seventeen," her mother said. "Some would say Sadie was past the age for getting married."

"But what would we do for a wedding?" Michiko felt saddened. *There would be no beautiful lace for a gown,* she thought. *There would be no yellow silk for bridesmaids.*

"I think we should just wait and see," her mother advised her. "So many things can happen."

"So many things can happen," Michiko repeated as she turned to the stove.

~ ~ ~

"It has to be someone from the Bachelor House," Kiko decided when Michiko told her about the picnic. "We should find out."

"How would we do that?" Michiko asked.

"We can follow her when she has another date and see who she meets."

"You mean spy on her?" Michiko looked at Kiko and blinked.

"Everyone thinks we are spies anyway."

"I don't know," said Michiko. "What if we get caught?"

"I never get caught at anything," Kiko said. As she said it a look of sly confidence darted across her eyes. Michiko was not sure why.

When Michiko came home from school there were clothes covering her mother's bed.

"It doesn't matter what you wear," Eiko was saying to Sadie.

"What do you think, Michiko?" Sadie asked when she walked into the room.

She held up her worn suit in front of her. "This makes me look like I am going to church." She flung it back on the bed, and picked up a pair of navy slacks. "If I wear these, I look like I work in a factory." Then she lifted the pale green outfit she wore the day they left Vancouver. "This used to be my best outfit, but it's so worn."

Michiko had never seen her aunt so worried. She didn't say it out loud, but Sadie would look good in a rice bag. Instead she asked, "Where are you going?"

Sadie slumped on top of the bed. "It's nowhere that special," she said. "How can it be? We aren't allowed to leave the area, no one has a car, and it's just …" her voice trailed off.

"It's just that you want to look special for the man-with-no-name," Eiko guessed. "Why don't you wear something of mine? My clothes haven't had an outing for a while."

"Could I?" Sadie said leaping up. "I'll take good care of whatever you lend me. I just need to wear something different."

Michiko looked through the doorway at her grandfather. Since his heart attack he spent his days sitting beside the window, gazing down at the garden. Once in a while, Mrs. Morrison would take him for a walk up to her house and give him a bowl of homemade soup.

"Why don't you tell Geechan?" Michiko asked. "Maybe it would cheer him up."

"Father wouldn't understand," Sadie said, lifting a brown-and-white-polka-dot dress with a matching jacket from a hanger. "When we were growing up we weren't even allowed to listen to a record player."

Michiko remembered the black leather box with shining handles that she got to open from time to time. When Sadie came to visit, the first thing she did was slide a vinyl disk from its brown paper sleeve and put it on the turntable. Sadie and her mother danced as they sang along with Bing Crosby. Michiko waltzed about with her baby brother in her arms. It all stopped when Geechan came to live with them. Or did it stop because the record player disappeared? She couldn't remember.

"Mr. Katsumoto loves to sing," Michiko told her.

"He does?" Sadie said in surprise.

"We sing 'Red River Valley' and 'Deep in the Heart of Texas' during music time," Michiko told her. "He's got a really good voice."

Sadie looked at Michiko and smiled. But this was a smile Michiko hadn't seen on her aunt's face in a very long time. It was the kind of smile made her eyes shine just like melting chocolate.

She must really like those songs too, Michiko thought.

Chapter Thirteen

THE HOSPITAL

The fallen maple leaves had blown all the way down to the lake. There was the kind of chill in the air that only comes when snow is right around the corner. Michiko didn't like hearing harsh cries of the geese as they passed across the sky.

Michiko's father had one arm in his coat when the knock sounded. He yanked the door open.

"I thought I'd check on the old fella," the doctor said, "on my way home."

"Please come in," her father choked out. "I was just heading up to your place."

The tall, heavy-boned, grey-haired man headed upstairs and into the kitchen. He pulled off his coat and placed it over the chair. The scrape of the chair across the floor woke Michiko's mother, who was sleeping at the kitchen table. She lifted her head from her arms.

Michiko looked at his black bag, thinking of all the horrible-tasting medicines that were inside. She followed the doctor to the doorway of the Geechan's bedroom, but he put his arm out to stop her from coming inside.

"A hot drink would be nice," he said.

Michiko returned to the kitchen and lifted the kettle from the back burner to the front. She waited for the kettle to sing, and then sprinkled a handful of black leaves into the pot. Their supply of green tea was so low that they saved it for Geechan.

Her mother and father sat with the cups in front of them, waiting.

Finally the doctor lowered himself into the round-backed wooden chair. Michiko pushed a steaming cup of dark tea toward him. He laced it with milk from the can with a white carnation on the front, took a sip, closed his eyes, and savoured it.

Michiko pried open the lid of the cookie tin and held it out to him. The doctor put his enormous paw inside and took out a small lump of oatmeal.

"I made them," Michiko bragged.

The doctor took a bite. "Delicious," he said.

"Well?" Michiko's mother asked in a hushed voice.

The doctor cleared his throat. "Your father needs to be in the hospital," he said. "The sooner the better. Not just for him but for you too, by the looks of it."

"The hospital," Michiko repeated. A lump the size of a rice ball came into her throat.

"I'll take him in my car," the doctor said, "if Sam will come with me."

Michiko's father helped Geechan get dressed. Around his frail, thin body, Eiko draped the quilt that he'd carried all the way from Vancouver.

Despite the cold, Michiko stood with her mother on the front porch to wave goodbye.

The next two days passed by quickly. Her mother performed her household tasks in silence. Mrs. Morrison visited every day, enveloping Eiko in her soft, warm arms.

When she pressed her warm cheek against Michiko's face, Michiko closed her eyes and fell into the smell of lavender shampoo.

After school on the third day, Michiko visited the small white hospital. Outside it was almost dark, but you couldn't tell in the hospital. The bright lights reflecting off the pale green walls made her feel like she was underwater. Noises of squeaking metal cart wheels, quiet conversations, footsteps on linoleum floors, and coughs surrounded her.

Her grandfather's thin parchment hands lay motionless across his chest on top of the sheets. "Geechan," she said, but he did not waken. Michiko shook him gently, but he did not respond. She took his hand, sending all of her love through a squeeze. Maybe this time he would turn his head to her and open his eyes. But he didn't. In frustration, she pinched his hand. He didn't even flinch.

At the sound of the train going by, Michiko looked up. For certain he would say, "Choo-choo," the way he always did to Hiro. But he didn't move or speak.

Michiko looked at her father leaning back in the chair with his eyes closed. When he slept he didn't have the same ghostly look to his skin that her grandfather had. "Why won't Geechan wake up?" she asked.

"He is in a very, very deep sleep," her mother told her as she entered the room. She looked at Michiko as if she was carrying a very sad secret.

"I'm not going to talk to him then," Michiko announced folding her arms across her chest, "until he opens his eyes."

"You must still talk to him," Sadie said, coming in behind Eiko. "He can still hear your voice." She leaned over and kissed the forehead of the man in the bed. "*Konnichiwa*," she said to him softly. "Are you in Japan?"

Michiko's mother looked up at Sadie in surprise. "I was thinking the same thing," she said with a sad smile. "I hope he's in his old neighbourhood with all his school friends."

Sadie placed her delicate hand on Michiko's shoulder. "He'd always planned to take you to Japan," she said. "He saved all his money in a cigar box. Geechan wanted you to know all about your culture and heritage."

Michiko remembered the thin wooden box with the white owl on the top. Her grandfather used to show it to her, tap the top, and say, "One day we go Japan."

She always dreamed about visiting the Land of Cherry Blossoms. She saw herself wearing a kimono, sitting on the floor at a low table to eat, and sleeping on a *tatami* mat behind a rice paper screen. Michiko wanted to see the mountain with the snow on the top that everyone drew and the crooked trees. But the stupid war got in the way and now Geechan wouldn't even wake up.

"He missed our mother," Sadie told Eiko. "He found her in you, but not in me."

"He found himself in you," Eiko told Sadie with a grin, "except for one thing."

"What was that?" Michiko wanted to know.

"*Yamato-damashii,*" her mother and aunt said at the same time.

Sadie laughed out loud. Her mother hid her laughter behind her hand.

Michiko glanced at her grandfather looking for a reaction, but there wasn't one.

"What is that?" asked Michiko, as Ted entered the room. "What is *Yamato-damashii*?"

"It means the true spirit of Japan," her uncle replied. He crossed the room and placed his large weathered hand on top of the two fragile weathered ones. Then he turned to Michiko. "It was one of the things your grandfather and Sadie fought about over and over again."

"That's not fair," Sadie said, turning to Eiko. "Ted fought with him too."

Michiko's eyes widened. This was news to her. She had never known a cross word to come between her grandfather and the three adults standing in the room. "You fought with your father?' she asked in awe.

"Yes, we did," Ted admitted. "Sadie and I had different dreams from the rest of the family. Especially Sadie. She only had only Canadian dreams."

Sadie gazed toward the man in the bed. "When he was young he followed all the Japanese ways. The Emperor of Japan was like a god to him," Sadie told Michiko. "He insisted your little brother be named Hiro, after the emperor." She walked over to Geechan and smoothed his brow. "After mother died he tried his best to make sure we stayed Japanese."

"Why didn't you argue?" Michiko asked her mother, even though she already knew her mother seldom argued with anyone. She just turned blank and moved away.

"Your mother knew how to be Japanese at home and Canadian at school. She lived in two worlds," her father said. "That is how it is with the oldest."

"Why does it have to be one or the other?" Michiko wanted to know. "Why can't we be Japanese and Canadian at the same time?

No one answered.

Late that night Michiko's father and mother returned from the hospital. Hiro was asleep, but Michiko lay in her bed reading.

Her mother gave out great sigh as she lowered herself on to the end of Michiko's bed. She took the book and folded Michiko's hands into hers. With bright eyes, Eiko spoke in a strained voice, "Sleep carried Geechan to his place of comfort."

Michiko nodded, she knew about his long deep sleep.

"He is there now," she whispered.

At first Michiko did not understand what her mother was saying. *Geechan was well enough to travel?* Then a cold fear crept around her heart as she realized what her mother meant. The entire inside of her body went hollow. The hurt swelled within her chest and came out in a great heaving sob.

Her father pulled her to him tight. Then he pushed her back, held her at arm's distance, and looked her straight in the eyes. "It's better where he is, I promise," he said in a soft, sad voice.

Chapter Fourteen

SAYONARA

Michiko put her feet on the cold linoleum floor and tip-toed to the window. The lacy frost on the glass shone like silver. Dense snow clouds covered the sky.

"It's freezing," she complained to her mother when she entered the kitchen. She couldn't count the number of times the cold had awakened her by making her legs and feet ache.

But her mother wasn't at her usual place in front of the stove. She sat on her bed, her back ramrod straight, staring at the wall. Her eyes sagged, her sorrow too deep for tears.

Michiko stood in the hallway with her arms about her waist. Her mother turned to her but didn't get up.

"This is the best I could do," Sadie said, entering the room holding two hats. "All I could find is some black feathers and netting." Her sadness gave her face the look of a china cup.

Michiko had no fancy hat to wear. Her navy straw hat blew off the day they rode in the back of Bert's truck. She had to be content with her mother's head scarf over her toque.

"What about Uncle Ted?" she asked.

Sadie looked up from adjusting the netting. "I hope he makes it before the snow hits," she said, furrowing her brow. "With all this wind, there will be huge drifts." Sadie put the two hats down and took Eiko's hand.

Michiko wandered into the kitchen and sat down to a bowl of cold porridge. Within minutes she washed her bowl, dried it, and put it back in the cupboard.

"He has to come," Michiko heard her mother say. "He can't miss his father's funeral."

"Ted will do the best he can," Sadie assured her. "But he is a long way away. We don't even know if Mrs. Morrison's telegram reached the lumber camp."

When Ted first told the family he was making shiplap, Michiko thought he was back to work in the shipyard. "Not ships," he corrected her. "Shiplap is the rough wood siding they use for houses around here. But I'm going to convince them to branch out into windows and doors."

Eiko's eyes brimmed with concern. "Will it be safe to drive in this weather?"

By noon the snow smothered the street. The drift at the back door was so large they were unable to open it. They went through the drugstore to the front door, where a new hand-printed sign hung over the doorknob: CLOSED FOR FAMILE FUNERAL. Her father had misspelled the word *family* but Michiko wasn't going to tell him. His cardboard MERRY CHRISTMAS sign in the window, spelled out in cotton balls, was perfect.

Outside Michiko lifted her little brother to her father's decorated window. Green crepe paper draped the window like an awning. Red net stockings filled with candy lay against boxes of chocolate-covered cherries and peanut brittle. Small tinfoil Santa statues stood in the centre.

Tomorrow she would take Hiro to the General Store. In their window a mechanical Santa Claus moved up and down, holding a pickaxe. All around him lay candies wrapped in silver foil.

~ ~ ~

The family made their way to the church at the top of the street, leaving footprints in the white. "Look, Hiro," Michiko said, sticking out her tongue. A fat snowflake floated onto her tongue. "It's ice cream." She held tightly to Hiro's hand, allowing the adults to move ahead. Nothing would stress her mother more than an incident of bad behavior.

Two turkeys hung head down in the window of the butcher shop. The sign below urged people to place their orders soon. Michiko thought about the deep layer of sawdust that covered the floor. At first she thought it was a wonderful way to freshen the shop's sour air, until Clarence told her it was there to catch drips of blood. Michiko wrinkled her nose and stamped the sawdust from her shoes all the way home.

A crowd of people stood around the heavy wooden doors of the church, speaking in low murmurs. There was talk of her grandfather's wonderful garden. Several came forward to shake hands with Michiko's family. Clarence led a tall man in a grey overcoat by the hand to Michiko.

"This is my father," he said to her with a crooked grin.

Michiko stared up at the tall man with grizzled ginger hair. He put out his hand and she shook it. Then he extended his hands to Michiko's mother and father. "My boy talked a lot about the old guy," he said, "may he rest in peace."

The thunder of a giant logging truck pulling up to the church made everyone stop and look. Over his blue jeans, Ted wore a navy topcoat and fedora. He reached for Sadie's arm. Michiko threw her arms about her uncle's waist.

Michiko breathed in the smell of wood polish when they entered the small white church with the yellow diamond windows. On the altar a vase held a single white lily. The old reed organ stood to the right of the pulpit. Michiko was surprised to see Bert's wife, Mabel, adjusting the sheets of music, wearing a black hat and coat. The minister wore a gold satin scarf with embroidered crosses.

Michiko flipped through the pages of the hymn book while the Mabel pumped the carpeted pedals. "Hiro," she said, in an attempt to keep him occupied, "tell me the numbers."

She pointed to the white cards in the wooden shield on the wall.

Everyone shuffled to their feet in order to sing. Mrs. Morrison's voice rose just slightly over the others. She held the notes just a bit longer than the rest of the people singing.

Hiro glanced up as if he had just remembered something. He looked around and then slid out of the pew to the red-carpeted aisle. "Geechan," he called out as if he was playing a game of hide-and-seek. "Geechan," he called again, walking down the aisle.

Several women raised gloved hands to their mouths.

Michiko darted after him just as Mr. Katsumoto stepped into the aisle. He scooped Hiro up and flipped him onto his shoulder. Michiko followed them to the church basement. There Mr. Katsumoto flipped Hiro back down to the ground.

Her teacher pulled out the bench and tickled the keys of the upright piano.

"I didn't know you could play the piano," Michiko said in surprise.

"Keeps my fingers nimble," he replied as he wiggled his fingers. "It's good for baseball."

Hiro ran across the shiny hardwood floor, skidded, and fell with a thump. Giant tears welled up in his almond-shaped brown eyes.

"Hey, little fella," Mr. Katsumoto said, "want to gallop like a horse?"

Michiko took off her coat, then undid the buckles and stepped out of the rubber boots she wore over her shoes. "Watch, Hiro," she said. "This is how."

Mr. Katsumoto played while Michiko galloped around the hall. With a smile, Hiro copied. "We have a piano at home," she called out across the hardwood space.

"It's a good way to wear the little guy out," Mr. Katsumoto said with a laugh.

"He's not so bad," Michiko explained. "But he does like to get into things."

"Sort of like your Aunt Sadie," he commented.

"Do you know her?" Michiko asked, stopping her gallop.

"All the teachers know each other," he said, grinning down at the piano keys.

Michiko looked at the smiling, handsome man. Her grandfather would have been proud to have Mr. Katsumoto as Sadie's boyfriend, a much better choice than the man-with-no-name.

Geechan's walnut face floated into her mind. He had a way of smiling that lit up his whole face. She could just see him shaking Mr. Katsumoto's hand, saying, *"Come-gratulations,"* over and over again, the way he misspoke English.

"Life goes on," people kept saying to her over and over again. *But if life went on,* she thought, *he'd be here right now.*

A great grey sadness seeped into her heart. Geechan had been such a big part of her life. He stayed at their house when the government took her father away. He rode the train with them, carrying the quilt full of money. He chopped wood and pumped water at the farmhouse and planted their gardens. At bedtime he showed her *Sode Boshi,* the kimono sleeve in the stars. Michiko didn't even get to say goodbye to her grandfather. A huge lump of tears filled her throat. *People should be saying that death goes on. Geechan will be dead forever.* She put her hand to her throat, making a strange choking sound.

Mr. Katsumoto stopped playing. "I'm so sorry," he said softly. "It is such a sad time."

Michiko nodded. The lump melted as tears streamed down her cheeks. She wiped them away with the cuff of her sweater.

Hiro raced to the piano and banged a few keys.

"Watch," Mr. Katsumoto said to him. "I'll show you how to play the galloping music."

~ ~ ~

As Michiko's family talked outside the church with Mrs. Morrison, Mr. Katsumoto surprised them all by carrying a sleeping Hiro toward them.

"Mr. Katsumoto played the piano!" Michiko exclaimed, "And he tired Hiro out."

Her teacher extended a free hand to her father and mother. "Please accept my condolences," he said. "He was a great baseball coach."

"I wish he could have gotten to know you better," Sam replied. "You were his hero."

"I'm not going to join you for dinner," Mrs. Morrison said in a wobbly voice. She put her hands on her chest as if to stop them from heaving. Her face was white and lined.

"We have already set you a place," Eiko said, but Mrs. Morrison walked away, wiping her eyes.

Sadie, joining the group, caught her breath at the sight of Mr. Katsumoto.

"We don't have to take her plate away," Michiko said, looking at her mother in earnest.

Her mother took the hint. "Would you care to join us?" she asked Michiko's teacher.

Mr. Katsumoto didn't respond at first, busy transferring Hiro to Ted's arms. "I wouldn't want to impose," he finally said, "under the circumstances."

"It would be an honour to my father," Eiko said. "He never stopped talking about seeing you win the Terminal League Championship."

At dinner Mr. Katsumoto entertained them with stories of his days in road camp. "We sat at a long table of green wood with two benches," he told them. "There were ten place settings, five at each side. Each of us had a tin pie plate and an enamel cup."

Michiko, seeing her father nod at the description, stared down at her rice bowl.

"One man chopped the green tops off the carrots," Mr. Katsumoto told them, "another put two on each plate."

"We ate a lot of raw as well," Michiko's father said. "Once all we had to eat was a wedge of cabbage.

Michiko looked up in surprise. Her father seldom talked about the time he was away.

"I could put up with the poor food and the isolation," Sam said. "The real torture was the blackflies." He reached over and patted his wife's hand. "My wife insisted I take a set of bed sheets."

Michiko's mother lowered her eyes in embarrassment.

"I used them to cover myself from the flies," he said. "At least there were no rats."

Michiko dropped her chopsticks.

Her mother rose from the table. "Thankfully we are all better off than that now," she said as she lifted the cloth from the plate of small round cakes in the centre of the table.

"You should have been at our house for New Years," Michiko said to her teacher. She closed her eyes and sighed. "Nothing tastes better than New Year's mochi."

"Aah," said Mr. Katsumoto, "I often dream about those sweet red bean cakes."

"It is so hard," Eiko said, looking at Sadie, "getting the right ingredients."

"But you've got a Christmas tree," Mr. Katsumoto said. "I haven't seen one in years."

"We should put a Christmas tree up at school," Michiko said, "for our class party."

"What class party?" Mr. Katsumoto asked in mock seriousness.

"The one you plan on giving your students," Sadie said with a large smile.

"Once I read a story about a family that had no money for decorations," Michiko told him eagerly. "A spider heard them and covered the tree with beautiful cobwebs."

"I try not to read too much these days," Mr. Katsumoto said to Michiko's surprise.

Sadie said in a soft voice, "I can't imagine living with someone who didn't read."

"I didn't say I don't enjoy reading," he replied. "With no books around, I get frustrated."

"You can read all of my books," Michiko said.

"Why thank you, Michiko," Mr. Katsumoto said, "but only one at a time."

Sam turned and spoke quietly to his wife, "Will you play the piano?

As the snow fell like petals from a cherry blossom, the Minagawa family sat with their guest and listened to her grandfather's favourite songs of Japan.

Chapter Fifteen

SPECIAL DELIVERY

"What's in the box?" Michiko asked her father.

He looked up from prying the lid off the wooden crate and shrugged. It took up most of the space at the bottom on the stairs. When he finally lifted the lid all they saw was straw.

"This really is a mystery," Michiko's mother observed. She put her hand out to stop Hiro from pulling out a great clump of yellow. "We need to unpack it properly," she announced. "The straw will be good for the garden." She shooed everyone back.

The first thing hidden beneath the straw was a cardboard carton labelled CONES.

"Ice cream cones," Michiko read in astonishment. "Who would send us ice cream cones? Don't they know we live above a soda fountain?"

Michiko's mother passed the box to Sadie. She shook it. "Too heavy for cones," she said.

The second discovery was a box of disposable diapers. Taped to the side were two blue panty covers. "Whoever sent it doesn't know Hiro has grown," Michiko observed.

"Whoever sent it," Sadie responded, "has money. Those cost about six cents each."

Next was a large box of detergent.

"Why send detergent with disposable diapers?" asked Sam. He chuckled at his own joke.

At the bottom lay a large brown envelope addressed to Mrs. Sam Minagawa.

Over a cup of steaming tea, Michiko's mother opened the envelope in front of them all. She pulled out a letter, a small blue envelope, a cheque, a card, and a photograph.

Across the top of the letter ran the words, THE IMPERIAL CONFECTIONARY COMPANY OF CANADA. "It's from Mr. Riley," she exclaimed, scanning it from top to bottom.

Finally Michiko knew who sent the box. Mr. Riley was her father's Vancouver boss.

"*Dear Mrs. Minagawa,*" her mother read aloud. "*I am sorry to report that we have had to fill the position your husband held in our company.*" She gave a loud sigh before continuing. "*Fortunately we knew of your location. I have forwarded a photograph from your husband's desk drawer and a money order for his outstanding commissions.*"

Michiko's mother turned over a dog-eared photograph of Sam, Eiko, Michiko, and Hiro. Her eyes took on a faraway look. "Every New Year we dressed up and went to Mr. Fujiwara's studio," she said, lowering the photograph into her table, "until it closed down."

Then she picked up the cheque and held it to her breast. Michiko dared not ask how much. Her mother placed it face down, lifted the small blue envelope, and opened it.

"*Dear Mrs. Minagawa,*" she read, "*My aunt isn't much for writing, but she did let me know you arrived safely.*"

She looked at the signature on the bottom. "It's from Paul Morrison, Mrs. Morrison's nephew."

She continued reading. *"I hope everyone is well. The staff put together some items we think you might like. We think of Sam often, Paul."*

Michiko's mother returned the blue paper to its envelope. The Christmas card brought them all greetings from the staff of the Imperial Confectionary Company.

"Now can we open the boxes?" Michiko asked in exasperation.

Her mother nodded and they rose from the table.

"This one first," Michiko said, indicating the ice cream cone box.

The carton contained a brown teddy bear. Its nose and the insides of its ears were golden brown. "It's so sweet," Michiko said giving it big squeeze. It surprised her with a squeak.

She handed it to Hiro. He clutched it with a wide grin.

There was a giant-sized package of coloured pencils, several orange scribblers, and a large puzzle of two kittens in a basket. At the very bottom lay a thick book. Michiko grinned.

Another carton held wool, knitting needles, and long rolls of digestive biscuits. There were tins of peaches, evaporated milk, and bags of candies that looked like tiny golden pillows.

Michiko squealed when her mother pulled out the box of candy canes.

"Candy canes," Michiko told everyone. "We have candy canes."

Michiko closed her eyes. Her thoughts drifted back to a once-upon-a-time Christmas in Vancouver. Stacks of presents sat beneath the tree in the corner of their living room. Christmas cards danced along the mantelpiece from a green ribbon. Special smells came from the kitchen.

Michiko opened her eyes. Last year all they had was a pine tree with paper ornaments stuck in a bucket of sand. This year they had candy canes!

Covered in red silk and dressed with a large black tassel, the last box was unlike any of the others. Her mother lifted the lid to reveal a thick wooden brush, an ink stick, an ink stone shaped like a cherry blossom, and a roll of rice paper.

Michiko rubbed her eyes. "Sadie," she called out, "look."

Sadie nodded. "The four treasures," she said with a smile.

Michiko suddenly remembered an elderly Japanese man saying those very words. Her art teacher at Japanese school called them *sumi*, *suzuri*, *fude*, and *kami*, Japanese for the ink stick, ink stone, brush, and paper. The Four Treasures were all you needed to paint.

"This is perfect," Sadie announced. "Next week we are starting special classes."

"What kind of classes?" Michiko asked.

Sadie lowered her voice and said, "The kind of classes that will probably cause trouble." She cupped her elegant hands around her mouth and whispered, "Japanese culture classes."

"Who's giving them?" Eiko asked.

"Whoever we can get," Sadie's said. "We are looking for talented people."

"Mr. Katsumoto could teach origami," Michiko told her aunt.

"How do you know that?" Sadie asked.

"He shows us stuff in class," Michiko replied. She pointed to the little blue vase filled with paper flowers. "Kiko taught me to make tulips but Mr. Katsumoto showed us the iris."

"He is a man of many talents," Sadie replied with a faint smile.

"You can teach dance," Michiko said.

"I plan to," Sadie said as she unrolled a pale yellow sheet of rice paper and grimaced. Tiny threads danced beneath the surface. "This paper is not as creamy as it should be." She sighed. "But it's not as if anyone can send away for better supplies."

"We should be grateful to have it," Michiko said as she filled the small well in the ink stone with water. If she remembered correctly it should only be half-full. She dipped one end of the ink stick into the water and then placed it straight up on the flat surface. She rubbed the ink, grinding down the stick. It ran down the sloping surface and mingled with the water in the well. It seemed to be right, but she wasn't sure. She had only done this with a master present. Michiko propped the stick on the edge of the stone. Everyone gathered to watch as she picked up the brush. She put it back down.

"We never painted on good paper first," she said. "We always started out on newspaper."

"I'll get one from downstairs," her father offered. They didn't keep newspapers in the upstairs apartment. Her mother had forbidden them.

Michiko dipped the brush into a small jar of clean water and wiped it on the side. She dipped the tip of the brush in the ink and took it to the newspaper. "I'm not good at this anymore," she mumbled looking at the bamboo leaf she tried to make.

"What did you say?" asked her mother from across the room.

"It is supposed to be art," Michiko complained, putting down the brush.

"Chokuhitsu," her mother called out. *"Chokuhitsu* and *sokuhitsu."*

Michiko nodded. She knew she was always supposed to practise the two basic strokes first, before trying to make anything else. That's all they ever did in class. They practised nothing but strokes, curved and straight, horizontal and vertical, thick and thin, and then circles. But Michiko, always impatient with these exercises, wanted to paint pictures.

Michiko sighed and put down the brush. "Too bad Uncle Ted can't teach carpentry," she said. "Remember Hiro's small wooden boat?"

The word *boat* suddenly made Michiko nervous. *Would George King tell the RCMP?* She pushed the thought to the back of her mind.

Chapter Sixteen

THE EXPEDITION

"Does everyone know where we are going?" Mr. Katsumoto asked the group of bundled children standing in front of him. Michiko's scarf, damp from her breath, smelled of wet wool. It covered her mouth like the others' and muffled their answers. "We will board according to your assignments," he said, stopping in front of the horse-drawn wagon.

The children looked at each other, not knowing what their teacher meant.

"First group," he announced, "are the Horsemen. You will drag the tree out of the woods." He read out four names. The four largest boys stepped forward.

Mr. Katsumoto opened his burlap sack. He placed a round object in each of their hands. "Every horse should have sleigh bells," he said.

The boys opened their hands and their eyes widened. With a grin they shook the small string of little gold bells. Mr. Katsumoto waved them over to the waiting wagon.

"Next group are the Woodsmen," he called out. "Your job is to identify and mark the best tree to cut down." He held up several long pieces of red ribbon. Kiko stepped forward when Mr. Katsumoto called out her name.

The Merry Men were to make merry music and sing. Michiko received a small tin flute.

Mr. Katsumoto gave each of the Axe Men a helmet of cork, but he carried the axes.

Michiko remembered this wagon when she climbed aboard. The old farm horses in their long straw collars and heavy traces often pulled it past the farmhouse. When the front wheel hit a bump, the load rattled. Once a few potatoes rolled from the top of the pile and landed on the road. Her grandfather leapt from his chair and ran down the steps. She could still see him waving away the dust as he bent down to pick them up. He walked back with pockets bulging. "Special delivery," he told her with a wink.

From then on, Michiko stopped and waited whenever the wagon passed by. Once it drove by piled high with crates. The strong smell told her it was cabbage, but nothing fell off.

Mr. Hayashi drove the horses along the old orchard trail into the forest. The snow-covered pines towered around them. It was still, almost tense with expectation.

"Let's have a song," Mr. Katsumoto shouted, "since we are dashing through the snow."

The boys with the bells began the chorus. Michiko and the others with the flutes joined in. Kiko sang out in her high tinny voice. In no time at all they arrived at the clearing.

Once the children were off the truck they started throwing snowballs. Kiko bobbed up and down, firing them quickly. She raised her arms in the air and stuck out her tongue, daring the boys to hit her. Michiko giggled until she saw a flash of gold.

"Let me see your bracelet?" she asked excitedly. "When did you get it?"

"My father bought me a watch for my birthday," Kiko said, tugging her jacket to cover it.

"Your father bought you a watch?" Michiko said in amazement. Kiko's birthday wasn't until the spring. "That was a generous of him," she said.

But Kiko wouldn't let her see it.

They walked to the rocky ledge. From where Michiko and Kiko stood, they could see the whole community of tiny wooden houses. Smoke rose straight up from the rows and rows of shacks. Some of the small children were out on the slope behind the old Apple Depot, sliding on rice bags.

"We still haven't had any news about Mrs. Morrison's husband," Michiko said.

"He's probably just floating around the ocean," Kiko said with a sigh. "D-E-A-D."

"What?" Michiko screeched. She turned to Kiko, her face red with fury.

"What I meant is," Kiko said, taking a step back, "it's not as if they have any children. It's not like he's someone's father."

"So what?" Michiko screamed. She picked up a great wad of snow and threw it at Kiko. "I would think you of all people would care about people going missing. How would you like it if your father went missing like your mother?"

As soon as the words spilled out of her mouth, Michiko wanted to take them back. The pale, ashen look that came over Kiko's face told her she had said the wrong thing.

Kiko brushed the snow from her shoulders without looking at what she was doing.

"I am so sorry, Kiko," Michiko cried, rushing to her side. She helped brush the snow away. Then she removed the woolen scarf from her own neck and wrapped it around Kiko's. "I think some snow got down your neck. This will keep you warm."

But Kiko did not reply. She stared straight ahead as if she had seen a ghost. Then she walked back to the wagon and took a seat. All the way back to the school she stayed silent.

The inside of the Hardware Store School seemed fusty compared to the fresh air of the forest, until they smelled the hot chocolate. Some of the mothers had made it as a surprise.

But the best surprise of all was the gift bag each child received from the Timothy Eaton Company. It contained a small bag of hard candies, an orange, a yo-yo, crayons, and a red kaleidoscope.

The giant pine breathed the delicious smell of Christmas into the whole building. They put fir boughs everywhere. Mr. Katsumoto tied a large spray of greenery to the school's front door.

~ ~ ~

All week long Michiko's class prepared decorations. Sadie supplied the class with soft white paper, scissors, and glue to cut snowflakes to spin from the ceiling. The class transformed the bleak dilapidated building into a Christmas hall.

Each day Kiko worked without a sound. Her tinny laugh never rose above the noise.

Mr. Katsumoto taught them how to make a wire handle and punch holes in a tin can for a lantern. Michiko worked diligently on a star pattern. Kiko worked on a heart.

Each time Michiko tried to apologize for the awful thing she said, Kiko just moved away to work at a different table.

Finally, Michiko went to her side and put her arm around her friend. "I really didn't mean what I said about your father."

Kiko looked up. "He's not my father," she said in a low voice.

At first Michiko thought she had heard incorrectly. After a long silence, she whispered, "What do you mean he is not your father?"

"He is my uncle," Kiko said. She laid her head across her arms. "I thought if I pretended he was my father, I might not miss my parents so much."

"Did your father go to Japan too?" Michiko asked.

Kiko dragged her bottom teeth across her lip before speaking. "My father refused to evacuate. He left me with his brother before he ran off. If they catch him, he'll go to jail."

She put her face down into her arms.

"Good thing you have an uncle to count on," Michiko said, patting her friend's back.

"Count on him?" Kiko said raising her head. "All he ever does is count on me. I'm counting on you to do this, he says. I'm counting on you to do that." She uncrossed her arms. "He counts on me so much I could be an abacus!"

Michiko had to smile. "My mother is baking Christmas cookies today," she said. "Why don't you come home with me?"

Kiko raised her head. "I've never made Christmas cookies," she said. She sat up straight. "Would I get to eat one?"

"You can eat mine as well," Michiko offered.

~ ~ ~

Hiro jumped down from his chair when the girls entered the kitchen. "Kiko," he said putting his arms in the air when she entered the kitchen, "horsie."

Kiko pulled him on to her lap. She bounced Michiko's little brother up and down.

"Faster," Hiro demanded.

Kiko bounced him up and down on her knee making his black fringe bob and as his eyes grow wide. It was then that Michiko saw Kiko's watch. A watch that looked exactly likes Mrs. Morrison's.

Chapter Seventeen

HATUSYUME

Michiko woke with a sense of anxiety, but she didn't know why. She reached her toes down to the heated brick wrapped in flannel at the end of her bed, but it was cold. Then it came to her: she needed to take a closer look at Kiko's watch.

In the kitchen an orange scribbler lay open next to her bowl. Beside the can of milk with two holes punched in the top lay a sharpened pencil.

"Did you dream last night?" her mother asked as she stirred the oatmeal. She seemed pale and there were hollows under her cheeks.

Michiko looked up in surprise. *How did her mother know?* She dreamt every night, mostly about Geechan. Not bad dreams, but ones where he was riding with her on the train, working in the garden, and walking along the river. He would always stop, look at her, and smile.

"You need to practise writing down your dreams," her mother explained. "All the people in Japan record their first dream of *Hatusyume*."

Michiko thought about last night's dream as she played with the pencil. In it she was playing baseball. Clarence was the pitcher and Geechan the catcher. The ball floated toward her in slow motion. She swung the bat and hit it. The ball soared over the lake and landed in her old backyard. She started to run the bases. When she got to third her legs turned hard. She looked down and they had become bats.

"Run home, run home," Geechan called out to her.

Michiko reached down and lifted one of her bat legs forward. She did the same with the other. Halfway home she was too tired to continue. She started to cry.

"Run home, run home," Geechan called to her from home base.

She desperately wanted to get to home base. She looked at her legs again — now she was wearing *geta*. She ran on the Japanese shoes, but when she got to home base Geechan was gone.

"What if I don't understand what it is about?" she asked.

"All the more reason to write it," her mother told her. "The meaning will come later."

"Are we moving back to Japan?" Michiko asked.

Her mother whirled about, her eyes flashing. "I am Canadian," she said in a loud voice. Her face was angry and red. "This is my country. It's not a question of going *back* for me."

"But Kiko says," Michiko began to say.

"Kiko says a lot of things," her mother snapped. "I have had enough of this silly talk." She brought the saucepan to the table and ladled porridge into the bowl. She lifted the can, poured a steady stream of yellow milk over Michiko's porridge, and slammed it down.

Things are so different at Kiko's house, Michiko thought. *She can speak her own mind, disagree, and even change the topic of conversation. Here no one is even interested in discussing my ideas. I am to speak only if spoken to first.*

Michiko picked up her spoon. She decided to tell Kiko to write down her dream as soon as their ink thawed. It was so cold at night that the bottles on the ledge beside the stove wouldn't be ready for an hour.

Every morning the boys and girls in Michiko's class left their little wooden huts so bundled they could hardly move. Long johns went under corduroy pants, flannel blouses under sweaters. With their hats down to their eyes and their scarves up to their nose it was hard to tell who was who.

To keep their minds off the harsh winter, everyone stayed busy. When they weren't sweeping frost from the floor or icicles from the roofs, they attended the forbidden classes.

Tamiko took lessons in *Ikebana*. Kiko became a champion in Japanese chess. Raymond carved a knife for opening letters and a wooden whistle from a tree branch. He bragged about his plan to carve an entire baseball bat.

"Since you are so interested in wood," Mr. Katsumoto said to him one day, "you can be in charge of feeding the fire." Everyone laughed because the black pot-bellied stove consumed cord after cord. Raymond scowled. From the look on his face this was not the job that he had in mind.

Michiko attended classes in *Haiku*, but her poems had to wait for the special rice paper in the red box at home. There was still no one to teach her *Kanji*.

Edna Morrison, caught up in all the activity, formed a War Relief Club. The women of the church held meetings at her house to knit socks and scarves.

"Come home with me today," Michiko told Kiko. "It's warmer there."

"I hope it is warmer in our new home." Kiko said as they put on their coats.

"You can't go back to Vancouver? You told me it was Ban City."

"Who said anything about Vancouver?" Kiko replied with defiance. "My father," she said with a stutter, remembering Michiko knew the truth, "got permission to move to Ontario."

"Ontario?" Michiko repeated. She turned and grabbed Kiko's shoulders. "Why?"

"I keep telling you we are going to get moved again," Kiko said, kicking at the snow as they crossed the street. "My father said this time he's going to decide for himself where he wants to live."

As they entered the apartment, Michiko overheard Mrs. Morrison say, "I've brought a few live things into the world myself, living on the farm."

Kiko froze in the doorway. "I won't stay for lunch," she said. "I'll just tell your mother my news and go back to school."

Michiko frowned. "We've got enough, don't we?" she asked her mother.

"Of course we do," her mother exclaimed. "Kiko take your coat off and sit down."

"I'll let you get on with your lunch," Mrs. Morrison announced, lifting her heavy black purse from the floor and placing it on the table with a thud. "I'm attending a luncheon at the King residence today. All the women of the auxiliary will be there."

"Do you mean George King's house?" Michiko asked in astonishment.

"That's right," Mrs. Morrison said. "You know George, don't you?" She turned to Michiko's mother. "He's such an overprotected boy. His mother won't even let him get wet."

Michiko and Kiko burst out into such uncontrollable laughter they had to escape to Michiko's bedroom. Since January, Hiro slept in Geechan's old room.

"She won't even let him get wet," Kiko repeated with glee. "He didn't tell his mother."

"Let's hope that's not the only thing he didn't tell her," Michiko whispered back. So far the RCMP seemed to know nothing about the boat. Hopefully he would keep his promise.

"Did you know that Colgate is the only toothpaste used by the Dionne Quints?" her father asked, sticking his head in the doorway.

"They live in Ontario, don't they?" Michiko asked.

Her father nodded, beckoning them to lunch.

"Kiko is moving to Ontario," Michiko announced as they all sat down.

"Are you?" her father asked.

"Yes," she replied. "We got special permission."

"I wonder what Ontario is like," Michiko mused as she lifted her soup bowl to her nose.

"We can't think of moving anywhere," Michiko's mother said in a voice that was sharper than usual. She looked into Sam's eyes and blinked, as if flashing a warning.

"Why not?" asked Michiko.

"Why move?" Her father said in a jovial way. "We live here for free."

"Everyone is going to have to move again," Kiko said. "My father says so."

"Why don't we move to Ontario too?" Michiko asked.

"Michiko," her father said in a deep voice. She knew she had angered him. Her stomach churned as her mother cleared the table in silence. Eiko's face told Michiko there was to be no more talk about moving.

Chapter Eighteen

GOOD NEWS

Eiko sprawled on her hands and knees across the kitchen floor, scrubbing. "I'm finished," she said as she held her hand out to Michiko. "Help me get up," she whispered, almost out of breath. Lately every one of her sentences ended in a whisper.

Michiko leaned down and grasped her mother's hands. The linoleum floor smelled of soap and wax.

Eiko pulled heavily and rose to her feet. She put one hand on the back of the chair and winced as she tried to stretch her back. "I think I may have overdone it," she said. She leaned heavily on Michiko before sinking into a chair. "Make some tea, please."

"Is it all right if Kiko and I make popcorn?" Michiko asked. "One of the bags in the store had a hole in it and Kiko talked the clerk into giving it to her for free."

"As long as you keep the floor clean," her mother told her. "I can't face it again."

When Kiko arrived, Michiko's mother took off her blue checkered apron. "I'm going to lie down for a while," she told them. "You can keep Hiro busy with your popcorn."

"Don't forget to shake the pot really hard," Michiko advised Kiko when the wild pinging sounds started. It always reminded her of winter hail against the windows. She left the kitchen to peek in on her mother and covered her with the patchwork quilt.

Kiko pulled a chair to the stove. "Hiro," she said, "stand beside me and watch."

The pot lid rose and a collar of fluffy kernels peeped out. Soon popcorn danced onto the stove and bounced to the floor. Hiro jumped from the chair. He picked up the puffs and ate them.

"How much did you put in?" Michiko asked when she came into the kitchen, seeing the puffs drop.

Kiko shrugged. "I don't know," she said. "I put some in and Hiro put some in."

Michiko scooped up the bag. Over half was gone.

"You've put in way too much!" she exclaimed as she turned down the burner.

The floor looked as snowy as the road outside.

Hiro darted about, stuffing his mouth. Broken kernels stuck to the clean linoleum.

"My mother just washed the floor," Michiko moaned.

The two girls scooped up popcorn and filled a bowl. Even though the stove was off, it kept on popping and dropping. In desperation, Michiko opened the cupboard under the sink and grabbed an empty rice bag. She stuffed it with popcorn. Now there was mess and waste. That would upset her mother even more.

"We can take some to my father," Michiko said, "but we have to clean the floor first."

~ ~ ~

A bicycle whizzed by the front window just as Michiko entered the drugstore. She recognized the man's khaki uniform and polished boots.

"Oh no!" Michiko shrieked. "The telegram man could be going to Mrs. Morrison's."

Sam, Kiko, and Hiro went to the window.

"I'm going to find out," Michiko announced, tugging on her boots and grabbing her coat from the peg. She ran out the front door as fast as she could through the snow.

The bicycle was leaving when she arrived at Mrs. Morrison's front porch.

As Michiko ran up the steps, a sob came from the open front door. She stepped inside as Kiko pounded up on to the porch behind her.

Mrs. Morrison sat on the stairs, her face in her hands. An open envelope lay at her feet.

Michiko went on her knees. "Mrs. Morrison," she said, "is it bad news?"

The woman removed her large fleshy hands from her face. Her nose was bright red.

"He's …" she said. Her voice cracked. She looked at them both with wide eyes.

Michiko and Kiko helped her to the sofa.

"Get her a glass of water," Michiko commanded as she retrieved the letter.

"I'll read it out loud," Kiko said when she returned from the kitchen. She snatched it from Michiko's hand and scanned the strips of typed print. "He was rescued from a lifeboat."

"Hurray!" Michiko yelled, handing Mrs. Morrison a glass. "Where is he?"

"He's in a naval hospital in London."

"That's right," Mrs. Morrison said, finally able to speak. "He will be able to come home on leave." She crossed her fingers. "Hopefully the war will be all over before he has to go back."

"I knew he would be all right," Kiko said to her. "I always said that to Michiko."

Michiko shot her a glance of disbelief while she patted Mrs. Morrison's hand.

"My mother will be here soon," Michiko said.

"I hope not," Mrs. Morrison said standing up. "It's too far for her to walk in her condition." She turned to Kiko. "You run back and tell Eiko to stay put." She turned to Michiko. "You tell Bert to bring his truck."

When Bert pulled into the laneway, Mrs. Morrison waited on her front steps holding a large wicker basket. "We are going to celebrate," she said.

Michiko peeked inside at the bag of sugar, package of butter, a lemon, and huge bowl of eggs. This really is a celebration, Michiko thought. Mrs. Morrison usually sells her eggs. There was enough there to buy herself a new hat.

Michiko's mother met them at the door.

"I think I feel a bit of a cry coming on," Mrs. Morrison said as she climbed out of the truck. "I don't know what I would have done if it had been different."

Eiko gave her a hug.

"I was so afraid he drowned at sea," Edna said. "I didn't think that at first, but I when couldn't find the watch he gave me it seemed like a bad omen."

Michiko's eyes widened. Kiko stared at the ground.

"I have searched the whole house. I opened drawers, emptied vases, and moved things about. One night I looked until two o'clock in the morning and still no watch," Mrs. Morrison said. "You must think I am a foolish old woman."

"It is never foolish to care about things you love," Eiko said putting her arms around her friend. "I'm sure it will turn up," she squeezed her friend's shoulders, "just like your husband."

That night Michiko watched Mrs. Morrison make them lemon curd. She sat her mixing bowl on top of a saucepan of boiling water. Into it she cracked six eggs and beat them well. She stirred in the sugar and butter, and then put her hand out for the lemon.

Michiko and Kiko had been taking turns holding it and smelling it. Michiko remembered how Geechan could never make the sound of the letter *L*. He would always call the bright yellow fruit a *"wemon."* Sadie said it the same way too, just to tease.

Mrs. Morrison cut the lemon in half and gave the girls the job of squeezing in the juice. Then they stirred until it got as thick as honey.

"Speaking of good news," Sam said when he came upstairs, "isn't it about time you shared our good news with Mrs. Morrison?"

"She already knows," Eiko said with a bit of a blush.

"But your daughter doesn't," Mrs. Morrison said.

"Doesn't know what?" Michiko asked. *Had her mother changed her mind about moving?*

"You'll be happy about one thing," Sam said, looking at Michiko. "You won't have to share your room. It will be Hiro's turn to share this time."

"Is Sadie coming back to live with us?" Michiko asked.

"No," her father teased, "we haven't met the person who will be living with us."

Michiko looked at each of them as the smell of the sweet pudding filled the air.

Kiko hit her in the arm. "Your mother," Kiko began, but stopped, seeing Eiko's face.

Eiko moved to Michiko's side and whispered into her ear.

"We're having a baby!" Michiko exclaimed.

That night Michiko lay in bed, wide awake. There was so much to think about: Kiko going to Ontario, Mrs. Morrison's missing watch, and now a new baby.

Chapter Nineteen

THE WATCH

Michiko opened her eyes the next morning and gazed about her room. The small black-spotted mirror attached to her bureau reflected the wooden cat Geechan had carved for her. She looked at the ceiling. Geechan made the paper lantern that covered the bare bulb. He was always doing something for them. She needed to do something special for him.

She remembered the baby. It seemed like she had just gotten used to carting her brother around and now he ran and climbed everywhere.

Then she remembered the watch. She rose and dressed quickly.

"Can I go to Kiko's house today?" she asked her mother.

Her mother was busy taking apart one of Mrs. Morrison's dresses. She cut a pattern from brown paper. After she sewed it together again, inside out, it would look like new. Eiko nodded.

Michiko put on both her sweaters, then her coat. Tugging her hat down over her ears she thought about what she was going to say. What if Kiko wouldn't co-operate?

The cold, sharp air bit her face as she made her way down the middle of the snow-banked street. The water below the bridge rushed beneath a cover of ice.

This is where she would usually meet Clarence. *Clarence would never take anything that didn't belong to him,* she thought. *He even returned the baseball glove given to him at the game.*

The wind howled about her feet as she made her way down the laneway that led to the orchard. Wisps of smoke floated up from the tiny snow-covered roofs. She gave three hard knocks on the door of the newspaper house.

"Hello, Michiko," Mr. Sagara said as he opened the door. The familiar acrid smell of printers' ink tugged at her nose. His dark hair stood straight up on top of his head, reminding Michiko of a brush. He held a blue-stained cloth in one hand.

"Is Kiko at home?" Michiko inquired.

"No," he said.

"She has something that I have to get back," Michiko said at the doorway.

Mr. Sagara indicated that Michiko should sit on a kitchen chair. He went back to his stool in front of the rows of type letters. Michiko stared at the mildewed walls.

Kiko danced through the doorway. "Hi, Michiko," she said. She put her hands over the small black stove and rubbed them hard. "What are you doing here?"

"I came to get something back," Michiko whispered. "Something you borrowed."

Kiko stared at her blankly. Then she shrugged her shoulders.

"I want the watch," Michiko said, pointing to her friend's wrist.

Kiko's eyes flicked open. Then they half closed and opened again.

Mr. Sagara rubbed his face, smearing ink on his forehead. *"Najii des'ka?"* he asked as he got off the stool and came toward them. "Do you have a watch?"

"She said it was just an old thing," Kiko hissed at Michiko. She turned to her uncle. "She doesn't need it. Mrs. Morrison's got a huge clock in her hallway."

Mr. Sagara fixed his dark eyes on Kiko. "Did Mrs. Morrison say you could have it?"

Kiko looked away.

"Did Mrs. Morrison tell you that you could have it?" he repeated.

Kiko bit her bottom lip. Her eyes sparkled with tears.

"Kiko was supposed to put it on the mantel, but she put it on her wrist instead," Michiko blurted out. "Mrs. Morrison doesn't know where it is."

Kiko stared at her in disbelief.

"Well, then," Mr. Sagara said, taking a deep breath, "give the watch to Michiko."

Kiko yanked back the sleeve of her sweater. She undid the clasp, removed it, and slammed it into Michiko's outstretched hand. She slumped on to the chair and crossed her arms.

"Well," Mr. Sagara said, "you have your *hakujin* watch back. You can go home now."

Michiko fixed her eyes on Mr. Sagara, wondering what to say. Suddenly Geechan's voice floated into her head. "Those who make the first bad move always lose the game," Michiko said to him before she opened the door.

Mr. Sagara blinked rapidly.

Michiko turned on her heel and left. All the way

home her eyes smarted. How could she and Kiko possibly stay friends now?

At the bridge, hearing the sound of tires on snow, Michiko moved to let the vehicle pass.

"Hey, there," Bert's voice called out to her. "What are you doing way out here?" He leaned across the seat and opened the truck door.

Michiko's hand went to her pocket. What if Bert found out she had Mrs. Morrison's watch? It took him a long time to accept the Japanese people living in his town. This could change everything.

"Hop in," he said. "I'm going to the General Store."

Michiko climbed into the truck, glad of the warm interior. "Thanks," was all she could say. Her mind was full of what to do next.

When she got home, Mr. Katsumoto and Mr. Hayashi sat at the soda fountain counter.

"What's the matter?" her father asked as she took off her hat. "You look upset."

"Snowball fight," Michiko said removing her boots.

"In a word," she heard Mr. Hayashi say, "dispersal."

"We've been uprooted for more than two years already," her father complained.

"If I can get work in Raymond, Alberta, they'll let me play in the Southern Alberta Sugar Belt League," Mr. Katsumoto said.

"You want to harvest sugar beets with a college education?" Sam replied.

"The evacuation ended the Asahi team," Michiko heard her teacher say as she mounted the stairs. "At least I'd get a chance to play."

Michiko was so frightened she could hardly walk. If anyone caught her with Mrs. Morrison's watch she couldn't imagine what would happen. She stuffed it inside a clean sock in her drawer.

She went to the kitchen where Sadie was saying, "We need a *majnai*. Remember what mother used to do? She put the scissors on the stove and the right answer popped into her head. She said it worked every time."

"I don't want to talk about it anymore." Eiko said.

"Not talking about it doesn't make it go away," Sadie said. "Prime Minister Mackenzie King said that the Japanese people who do not move east will be sent to Japan."

"And how does he expect them to get there?"

"Oh, don't worry, he's thought of that," Sadie said with a laugh. "He's going to give each of us $200.00 for travelling expenses."

"We can't go anywhere with a baby on the way," Eiko said.

"Everyone has to pick up their pieces and move on."

"What pieces? There are no pieces of furniture, no car, no money for a house. Why leave with nothing to nothing?"

"Your family still has to move ahead," Sadie warned her. "You can't let this baby keep you back." Sadie lowered her voice. "Even Kaz is leaving."

"What?" Michiko screeched, unable to be invisible any longer. "Mr. Katsumoto is leaving?" She ran to Sadie. "He can't leave. He's our teacher."

Hiro, playing on the floor, saw Michiko's distress and began to wail.

Sadie stooped to pick up Hiro. "Now, now," she said. "Your father and Uncle Kaz will wonder what is going on up here."

"Uncle Kaz?" Michiko repeated. "Why did you call him that?"

"Because," Sadie said, "if he leaves I am going to have to go along with him as his wife."

Chapter Twenty

PUSSYWILLOWS

"Brush your hair," her mother said, tapping on Michiko's bedroom door. "We're having visitors today."

Michiko lay on top of her bed thinking how she could return Mrs. Morrison's watch without anyone knowing. She had no idea.

Her mother stepped into the doorway of Michiko's bedroom. Her face looked like the sun in all its fullness. "Hurry up," she whispered. "They will be here in a minute."

"It must be a girl," her father had told her the night before. "Your mother looked like a chubby pigeon with you. Her cheeks wobbled when she laughed." Hearing this, Michiko realized she hadn't heard her mother laugh in a long time.

Michiko barely had time to straighten her bed when Kiko arrived with her uncle. She had no idea what to say, but it didn't seem to matter. Kiko acted as if nothing had happened.

Her mother sat listening as Mr. Sagara told her their plans. A long package wrapped in newspaper lay across his lap.

"You have been so good to Kiko," Mr. Sagara told them both. "She talks so much about your family. I know she is sorry to leave." He glanced at Kiko, but she just stared at her feet.

"You are very fortunate to be leaving," Eiko replied. "When do you go?"

"The day after *Haru Matsuri*," he said. "We wouldn't want to miss the festivities." He looked at Kiko and smiled. "Kiko has been practising quite a lot for her performance."

"Thank you for printing out the posters," Michiko said to Mr. Sagara.

He nodded and smiled. The Japanese community was having their first spring festival, even though everyone in town called it a bazaar. The teachers and children had transformed the bleak school building into a showcase celebrating their winter accomplishments.

"It is time to move on," Mr. Sagara said, "too much looking in the rear-view mirror."

This is all that everyone talks about these days, moving forward, moving backward, Michiko thought. *Her family didn't talk about moving anywhere.*

"Do you have family in Toronto?" Michiko's mother asked.

Kiko turned her head and looked at the piano.

"We will be making enquiries as to the whereabouts of my brother," Mr. Sagara said. He stammered, "Kiko's uncle may be there."

Michiko's heart skipped a beat.

Kiko looked up at the ceiling.

Mr. Sagara looked at the package on his lap and blinked as if he saw it for the first time. "Forgive me," he said picking it up. "We thought you would like these."

He rose and attempted to put them in her mother's lap, but her mother had no lap.

Michiko rushed to take the bundle.

"Thank you very much, Mr. Sagara," her mother said. "That was very kind of you."

Placing it on the floor, Michiko pulled away the paper, revealing several long branches of pussy willows.

"We picked them this morning," Kiko said kneeling on the floor beside her. She stroked one of the tiny grey puffballs with her finger. "Feel how soft they are. If you put them in water they will root," she said.

Michiko lifted the bundle. "Let's do it," she said in a soft voice. What Kiko did was very wrong, but she couldn't stay angry at her.

"Do you think your father is in Ontario?" Michiko whispered to her in the kitchen.

Kiko shrugged. "Who knows," she said placing a stem into the jar of water.

There was a knock on the back door. Kiko and Michiko rushed to the landing. The two RCMP officers from down the street waited at the bottom of the stairs.

Michiko and Kiko strained to hear. But Sam led them into the drugstore.

"Will your family have to go back to Japan?" asked Kiko.

"There is no back," said Michiko, repeating her mother's words "We were not born in Japan." But she shivered, knowing that her mother would have to go wherever her father did.

Michiko watched Kiko and Mr. Sagara leave from the window. Mr. Sagara bent and scooped up a handful of pine needles. He stood for a moment, holding them in his hand as if he had never seen them before. Then he threw them to the ground.

~ ~ ~

That night Michiko woke to the sound of her parent's angry voices and went to their bedroom door.

"How will we establish a livelihood?" her mother asked. "It is a foreign country."

"It is my homeland," her father said in a quiet voice.

Michiko left her bed to peek through the space of the partly closed door.

"You have a bedridden mother and an elderly father," her mother said. "They will not wish to be burdened with an infant and two children."

"We will just have to pack up what we brought," her father said. He reached out to stroke her mother's cheek but she waved him away.

Michiko closed their door softly. She didn't want to hear anymore. *We brought Geechan,* she thought, *the only one in the family who wanted to go back to Japan.* Michiko no longer wanted to think about the Land of Cherry Blossoms.

~ ~ ~

The mud on Clarence's boots was evidence that he had carried the posters all over town. "I put one up in every window," he said, nodding toward his bundle. Two rolls of paper with large brown elastics stuck out from under his arm.

Clarence pulled out a poster, shook it, and let it unwind. Cherry blossoms danced around each corner. The words *Haru Matsuri* floated across the middle.

Michiko climbed up on to the window ledge to pull down a sign. Dust and dead spiders filled the bottom of the window. "This place really needs a spring cleaning," she said. Then she had the most brilliant idea.

Mrs. Morrison cleaned her house from top to bottom each spring. She told them she would be cleaning out the grate and polishing the brass fireplace screen next week. If Michiko dropped the watch into the ashes, she would be sure to find it.

"Let's go visit Mrs. Morrison," she suggested after sticking up the poster.

Chapter Twenty-One

HARU MATSURI

Michiko finished taking apart one of their white cotton pillowcases. So far there was a modest layette of four hand-made kimonos, a dozen hand-hemmed diapers, and four threadbare shirts that both she and Hiro had worn. A small knitted sweater, bonnet, and booties arrived from Sadie.

She glanced at her mother leaning back in the chair, her eyes closed. Michiko fluffed her pillow. *Thank goodness her father took Hiro out earlier,* she thought.

At her mother's sigh, Michiko looked up. "I don't have to go," she said, even though she couldn't wait for the festivities to begin.

"Go," her mother said. "Enjoy yourself."

In a cloud of flowery perfume, Sadie entered the room. "Look at this," she exclaimed lifting her lapel. "It's Pegasus," she said removing the mythical flying horse to let them examine the emerald green wings. "Kaz said it reminded him of me."

"The right man for you would never try to clip your wings," Michiko's mother said as she picked up her darning basket.

After an uncomfortable silence Sadie cleared her throat. "It won't be for long," she said. "After a year in the beet fields, we'll have enough for a home."

Michiko took a deep breath. "I wish I knew what we were doing," she said.

Her mother held her needle in the air and frowned. "That decision has not been made."

"I heard you talking about Japan."

"If you heard that you must have been eavesdropping." She wagged the needle back and forth. *"Yancha,"* she said.

"How else would I know what is going on?" asked Michiko. "You never tell me anything. Even Kiko knew you were having a baby before I did."

"Kiko knows more than she should for a girl her age," her mother commented. She cut the wool thread with her scissors and slipped the wooden mushroom out from the toe. She turned to Michiko. "It is not your worry," she said. "You will go where we go."

"You mean stick to kid business — that's what you mean," Michiko said stomping down the stairs and all the way across the street.

The school, decorated with paper lanterns and flowers, hosted a tea room, bake table, and a hot-dog stand. Tables displayed everyone's poetry, origami, wood carvings, and sewing. Michiko walked through it all and then made her way down the street to the hall that the old timers called the Opera House.

She picked her way through the crowd gathered on the front lawn. George leaned against the doorway, while his mother chatted with the other town women. Mrs. Morrison wore her new inside-out dress with a lace collar. Her gold watch sparkled on her wrist. Her straw hat, full of cherries, was perfect for the occasion.

The look on George's face told Michiko he really didn't want to be there with the ladies. Michiko smiled and waved at him — after all, he hadn't told about the boat.

The performances were taking place in the large, dimly lit hall with a stage at one end. Her father and Mr. Katsumoto set out every chair they could find and made benches of bricks and planks. The tiny cloakroom would serve as a change room for the dancers. All month long people had borrowed and traded kimonos, scarves, and fans.

George slid into the seat she had saved for Clarence. "Were you waving at me?"

But before Michiko could answer there was a loud bang from a drum. Michiko blinked at the sight of Mr. Yama dressed in a short dark *hanten* with red calligraphy marching down its lapels. Two thick wooden sticks hung below his cuffed sleeves. A white bandana with a large red sun crossed his dark brows. He stood glaring at the crowd from behind a giant wooden drum.

Michiko could hardly believe her eyes. Mr. Yama always stomped about in old shirts, baggy pants, and thick-soled shoes, even on hot days.

As master of ceremonies, Mr. Hayashi stepped in front of the crowd wearing his best blue suit. "On behalf of the community," he announced, "I welcome you to our very first Spring Festival." He waited for the crowd to settle. "We will begin with," he paused to look at his notes, "*Sakura, Sakura*."

The audience applauded as a young man took his place at the piano at one end of the stage. After his first piece he played a rousing rendition of "Deep in the Heart of Texas."

George grinned and clapped. "That's my favourite song," he said.

Michiko was glad he didn't comment on the first piece.

"*The Happy Dance of the Doll Festival* follows the piano performance," Mr. Hayashi announced. Behind him a group of girls scurried to their positions, holding their kimono sleeves close to their chests.

Mr. Yama moved to a small table beside the piano. He cranked the handle of the record player, lifted the needle arm, and put it on the disk. Scratchy Japanese music filled the room.

The girls nodded and pointed their fans. They dipped as they opened their fans at the same time. As they moved about the stage they fanned their faces. Then, resting their elbows on the delicate painted paper fans, they stopped and snapped the fans shut.

One by one Michiko examined the faces of the dancers. Kiko was not one of them. *What had she been practising?*

Placing their fans in the large wide belt about their waist, the dancers formed a circle. Each movement was gentle and well-practised. The girls scurried away to loud applause.

Mr. Hayashi announced, "The next dance is the story of a young woman having to say goodbye to her loved one." He gave such a magnificent sigh he made the audience laugh.

George held his fists to his face and hunched forward.

A woman in a snow-white kimono with a chalk-white face and cherry lips stepped into view. Garlands of small flowers fell from a comb of jewels in her hair. A folded parasol rested in the crook of her arm. The golden embroidery in her sash sparkled.

Once again, Mr. Yama operated the record player. But this dancer soon made them forget its tinny sound.

She brought the sleeve of her kimono to her brow, to reveal its bright green insides. With knees gently bent, she made sliding motions across the floor, dipping and swaying side to side. Her high wooden clogs made her delicate steps all the more spectacular.

With her head slightly bent, she paused with fingers to her chin. It was that movement that told Michiko it was Aunt Sadie.

Sadie opened her parasol and raised the beautiful painted chrysanthemums above her head. She moved in a circle, her sleeves floated beside her. She spun her parasol as she dipped. Everyone in the room knew she was happy.

As the tone of the music changed, Michiko's aunt placed her parasol on the floor and pulled a long silk scarf from her sleeve. As she moved she wrapped the scarf about her neck. She brought the ends up to touch her cheeks, as if she was wiping away giant tears. In a flash she undid the scarf, then let it flutter and drop.

Sadie brought one long sleeve of her kimono to her brow as she extended her other arm out, palm down. Her sense of despair was so great, Michiko wanted to run to her and hug her.

The dance ended when she sank to her knees behind the parasol.

At first no one made a sound. The thunderous applause made Michiko turn to see just how many people were watching. Not only was the whole orchard in attendance, almost all of the townsfolk were here as well. Clarence stood in the doorway with Mr. Katsumoto. But it was Mr.

Katsumoto's face that caught Michiko's eye and made her stare. He was wearing a look she had never seen before.

The activity at the front drew Michiko back to the show.

Mr. Yama brought his *taiko* into the centre. Three young men and a small boy came on stage. Each wore a short black *hanten* with a white bandana across their forehead. The young men placed their drums onto cross-legged stands. The small boy sat on the floor with his drum in front of him.

Mr. Hayashi rose and read from his notes. "This musical piece," he said, "is inspired by the clock works and the puppet master. It promises to be full of life and energy."

The audience moved about in their seats in anticipation. Drumming always brought excitement.

Mr. Yama tapped the side of his drum with the ends of the thick wooden drumsticks, making a clacking sound. Then he lunged at his drum, giving it one enormous bang.

George almost jumped out of his seat.

Each of the drummers hit their drums with force. The room throbbed with the clack of wooden sticks. It was as if they were all inside Mrs. Morrison's big hall clock. Michiko couldn't take her eyes off the fierce little drummer in the front.

"Wow," George said, "that little guy can really play."

Michiko covered her laughter with her hands, shaking her head.

George furrowed his brows and looked again. His eyes opened wide as it dawned on him. It wasn't a boy on the drums, it was Kiko.

Chapter Twenty-Two

TADPOLES

Michiko, Kiko, and Hiro all crouched, pushed aside the grass, and peered into the murky water. Dragonflies skirted the scum on the pond in the middle of the baseball diamond. Michiko could almost taste the slime.

Kiko took Hiro's stick and stirred. The tadpoles swarmed to the edge. As they wriggled, they could see their short stubby tails and front legs.

"Don't get dirty," Michiko warned Kiko. Her feet looked so dainty in running shoes painted with white polish. She wore her woollen coat wide open and carried a cardboard purse.

Kiko plucked at the collar of her blue nylon dotted-Swiss dress. "It's prickly."

Hiro picked up another stick.

"I should have brought a jar," Kiko said. "I could take some tadpoles with me."

The quiet pond reflected the sky and the clouds above them. Michiko's reflection rippled alongside Kiko's. They waited for Mr. Sagara to finish his business across the street at the RCMP office. All their paperwork had to be in order before they left. The security truck was making a special trip to the train station in the next town. Mr. Hayashi had invited Michiko and Clarence to go along for the ride.

They never spoke about Mrs. Morrison's watch. After Michiko congratulated Kiko on her tremendous drumming, they both acted as if nothing had happened.

Michiko spotted her parents coming down the street to say goodbye. They joined them as Eiko and Sam were shaking Mr. Sagara's hand and saying they were sorry that he was leaving.

"With all your newspaper experience, you should be able to find a job," Sam said.

"Kiko will have a chance for a much better education," Eiko commented.

Kiko stood beside her uncle's rope-tied cardboard suitcase, wearing a false smile.

"This is for you," Michiko's mother said as she handed Kiko two green plastic bows attached to a cardboard strip. Kiko removed them and Eiko fastened them to either side of her head. Kiko touched the barrettes with the tips of her fingers and smiled. "Thanks," she whispered.

Clarence arrived carrying a package of brown paper and string. He handed it to Michiko. "Arrived just in time," he said. Then he took Hiro's hand.

Hiro looked up and down the street. "Choo-choo," he said. "Choo-choo?"

"It won't be stopping here," Clarence said. "Kiko has to go to the next station."

It had been over two years since Michiko travelled the road from the railway station. This time she was sitting on a bench, instead of standing beside a pile of luggage in the open back of Bert's farm truck.

One side of the road was mountain, the other, lake. After they passed the RCMP guardhouse, Michiko tried to count the number of *S* turns in the road, but gave up after fifty-four. The mountaintops disappeared for a few moments into the clouds. There were patches of snow and signs warning them of avalanches. She hoped Mr. Hayashi would steer clear of the rocks on the road. If they got a flat tire, Kiko would miss her train.

A logging truck, loaded with red-barked cedar logs the size of truck tires, passed them on the road. "That's the company Uncle Ted works for," Michiko told Clarence.

But Clarence wasn't listening. His head stuck out the back. He craned his neck in all directions, the wind whipping his hair into frenzy. "My pa said there were hot springs around here." He turned to Michiko and smiled. "Sorta like a Japanese bath, I guess."

The train whistle echoed through the valley and turned the curve as they pulled into the station. Michiko handed Kiko the package. "We know you like to collect facts," she said as the steam from the coal-eating train billowed about them. "You can make a book about Toronto."

A little smile lifted the corner of Kiko's mouth. "I will keep a Commonplace Book."

"It won't be very common if it's a record of your life," Clarence said with a grin.

They beamed at each other like the friends they used to be.

Kiko held the package to her chest. "Someday we will look at it together," she said to Michiko. There seemed to be hope in Kiko's words, but Michiko didn't believe her. The chances of her family leaving town were as slim as a ghost.

Mr. Sagara picked up the two suitcases and boarded the train. They watched him and Kiko make their way down, inside the car. Kiko sat by the window opening and closing her fingers as a wave. She stretched her lips across her teeth in a brief smile.

The conductor picked up his little step and put it back inside the car. As the train lurched forward and pulled out of the station, it started to rain. Clarence and Michiko waved madly until it was just a puff of smoke in the distance. Michiko wondered what it was like in Toronto. *Would Kiko be able to go into the stores and be served by the clerks? Or would it be like Vancouver?*

It was a cold journey home. The rain drummed on the body of the truck. It was a good thing there was room for them in the front. The wipers scraped away the sheet of water on the windscreen. *Everything is ending*, Michiko thought. Their iris had wilted into a dark, slim, snarl. Mrs. Morrison's beautiful lilacs turned brown and shrivelled. Sooner or later the whole town would shrivel up and be gone.

George King waited in front of the drugstore on his bike. His curly hair needed a cut. It blew about his eyes. "Did your drummer friend get on the train?" he asked Michiko.

"That's right, George," Clarence answered. "Kiko's on her way to Toronto."

"Toronto," George repeated. "She's going to Toronto?"

"Yup," said Clarence. "And she has invited us to come and visit whenever we want."

Michiko looked at Clarence and frowned. Kiko didn't say that.

"Lucky her," George said mounting his bicycle. "All the way to Toronto." He put his foot on a pedal and pushed down hard. He was halfway up the street when Michiko's father unlocked the front door. Mr. Hayashi nodded to the two of them as he left.

"Did that boy want something from the store?" her father asked with a hint of worry in his voice. "I only closed for a second."

"I don't know," said Michiko, wondering why her father locked the door.

Michiko turned to Clarence. "You know, next time we go fishing," she began.

"I know what you are going to say," he said rolling his eyes. "You want me to invite George to come along."

Michiko nodded.

"He won't come," Clarence said. "You know he can't swim and his mother wouldn't let him."

"Why does his mother have to know?" she replied, knowing full well it would not go over well with her own mother if she heard what she just suggested.

"Michiko," her father shouted down from the top window.

"Yes, Father?" she replied. Now he was upstairs. *What was going on?*

"It is time."

"Okay," she replied. But it took her a few minute to understand what he meant. Her stomach jumped with excitement. "Okay," she said again, louder. She gave Clarence a wide smile and tore inside and up the stairs. Michiko remembered her mother saying her back felt funny the night before.

Her father stood with her mother at the apartment door. Michiko saw a tiny drop blood on her lower lip, as if she had bitten it. Michiko picked up her mother's small *furoshiki* and ran ahead to open the door downstairs. Eiko grimaced as they stepped off the porch, but never made a sound. All they had to do was get to the doctor's house. He would drive them to the hospital.

Michiko walked about the apartment, not sure what to do next.

"Yoo-hoo," called a familiar voice from the bottom of the stairs. "It's me."

Mrs. Morrison stood below, grinning. "Clarence came to tell me," she said with glee.

"Would you like a cup of tea?" Michiko asked, calling down the stairs.

"I'm not coming up," Edna replied. "I'll take Hiro back, to help feed the chickens."

"Poor chickens," Michiko thought as she buttoned her little brother's coat. *"Niwatori?"* she said to Hiro and smiled. "Are you going to feed the chickens?"

Hiro looked up. She wiped his morning porridge from his chin and helped him down the stairs. Then she turned the sign on the door to Closed.

~ ~ ~

"It's a girl!" Sadie cried, bursting into the kitchen just as Michiko finished the dishes. "A beautiful baby girl. Your father called the school."

"I have a baby sister?" Michiko said in astonishment.

"Don't you want to see her?" Her aunt shooed her toward the door. "There's an RCMP officer waiting in his car. He said he'd drop us off at the hospital."

Michiko's new baby sister was the smallest person she had ever seen. Her head was no bigger than a grapefruit. She had chubby red cheeks and fine black hair that shot out in all directions. Her small pink hands clenched either side of her face. As she pushed one of her tiny fists into her eye, Michiko's mother drew it away.

"She looks like Sadie," Michiko whispered.

"That's what I thought," her mother whispered back. Her dark eyes looked tired and she smelled of medicine.

"Perfect in every way," said the nurse entering the room, "a very healthy child."

"Would you like to hold her?" asked her mother.

"I guess," Michiko said with a grimace.

As she cradled the tiny bundle in her arms the sweet smell of talcum powder drifted up. Michiko bent to kiss her soft round cheek and caught the smell of brand-new skin. A tiny fist opened. Michiko slipped her finger into it. Five tiny pink fingers closed over it. A shiver started at her fingertips and went up her arms.

"Lucky girl," the nurse said arranging the pillows behind Eiko's head.

"I guess I am," Michiko responded.

"I meant the baby," the nurse said. "I always wanted a big sister."

That night Michiko paused over and over again while reading in bed. She couldn't concentrate. Her sister's tiny face kept appearing on the page. Then she heard a sob.

Michiko put the book down and tiptoed to her brother's doorway. He was fast asleep. She heard the noise again. It came from the kitchen.

Her father, his head buried into his hands, was shaking.

"What's wrong?" Michiko cried out. "Did something happen to the baby?"

Her father took his hands from his face and looked at her. "The baby is fine," he said.

Michiko slipped into the chair beside him and put her arm around him.

"You must forgive me," he said. "There is so much to worry about these days."

Michiko patted her father's arm. "There is nothing to worry about," she said. "Remember what Geechan always said: at the foot of the lighthouse it is always dark."

"Not if the lighthouse is in Japan," her father replied.

"I don't know what you mean," Michiko said, a tinge of fear creeping into in her heart.

"I mean," he stammered, running his fingers through his hair, "before your little sister was born, Mr. Hayashi helped me fill out the papers to send our whole family to Japan."

Chapter Twenty-Three

THE LETTER

"I'm glad you know the difference," Clarence said to Michiko in their back garden. "I'm never sure what are weeds and what are vegetables." He scraped his hair back from his freckled forehead and stuffed it under his baseball cap.

Michiko picked up her rake. "Hello," she said to Mrs. Morrison, who was walking toward them.

"How's the new baby?" was the woman's first question every time they met.

"Fine," Michiko said with a smile.

Clarence and Michiko set to work weeding.

Mrs. Morrison talked as they worked. "There hasn't been a baby around here in a long time," she said. "All kinds of kids used to run up and down the main street."

"Now there's only George King," Clarence said in an aggravated tone. "George King, King of the Town, as he likes to say."

Michiko giggled.

"Poor George," Mrs. Morrison said, inspecting the beds.

"Poor George?" echoed Clarence in astonishment. "He's the richest kid around."

"George is poor in other ways," Mrs. Morrison told them. "He is poor in health, poor at sports, and he is poor at making friends."

"Maybe because he is a poor sport," Clarence said giving a dandelion a swift slash.

"George King was the only child of the King family to survive," she said.

Clarence, having seven brothers and sisters, looked up in astonishment.

Michiko blood turned cold. She opened her eyes wide.

Edna Morrison read the fear in Michiko's eyes. "Not that it's a problem for a healthy baby girl like yours," she assured her.

"How many children did she have?" Clarence asked.

"Three before George," said Mrs. Morrison. "There were two girls and a boy. They never lived past their first year of life. All of them are in the church cemetery."

Michiko thought of the small angel statues in the children's section. She shivered. If there was one place in the whole area that Michiko disliked, it was the cemetery. Halfway down the mountain between the farmhouse and the orchard, it was a tangled mass of wildflowers and weeds. The little iron-railed plots with gulls crying overhead made her uneasy. Trying not to think of it, she raked with gusto.

"George was the only one to live past his first birthday," Mrs. Morrison told them. "His mother was unable to have more children."

Clarence and Michiko listened as they scratched out the weeds around the vegetables.

"George's mother and I went to school together," Mrs. Morrison said as she did up her cardigan buttons. "Kathleen was the only girl from a well-to-do family of boys. Her mother dressed her in frills every day."

"Sometimes I wish I was an only child," Clarence said. "Our house gets real noisy at times and we are always running out of food."

"But you would be lonely," Michiko said. She couldn't imagine not having Hiro around. He got into things but she loved him. "And you'd end up being self-ish," she added.

"Being an only child doesn't make you selfish," Mrs. Morrison said indignantly, putting her hands on her hips. "I was an only child. But instead of wearing frills, I had to work the farm. I had to keep the chickens, milk the cows and the goat, and tend to the gardens. I used to wash my face in goats milk trying to look as pale and pretty as Kathleen."

Michiko looked up at the woman's red shiny face gleaming in the sun. One couldn't find a more kind and generous woman. "You don't need goat's milk," she said dropping her hoe. She threw her arms around Edna's waist and buried her face in her cardigan. "You are beautiful."

Taken by surprise, Edna Morrison's eyes widened. Then they softened and turned moist. "I think you are beautiful too," she said stroking Michiko's dark head.

"Doesn't anyone think I am beautiful?" Clarence asked, leaning against his shovel with his cap shoved to the back of his head.

Michiko released Mrs. Morrison with a giggle.

"Time for my visit," the woman announced, heading in the door.

Michiko bent to straighten the rickety peony cage, fashioned out of rusty fence wire. The scraggly plant trapped inside looked limp. "Maybe we should try to make friends with George."

"How?" asked Clarence. "His mother won't let him play with me. I'm from the wrong side of the tracks. And you are ..." But he stopped talking.

"I am an enemy of the country," Michiko finished for him. "I come from a whole family of spies." She remembered what Kiko had said once about being a spy. "Maybe," she said, "we could do it in secret. Isn't that what spies do?"

"He'll only cause trouble," Clarence said. "That is the one thing he isn't poor at." He stopped raking and rested his chin on the handle. "Why don't you invite him to the wedding?"

Michiko threw a dandelion plant at him.

The wedding was producing as much excitement as the summer baseball games. Mrs. Morrison organized the church women into cleaning every inch of the chapel.

Before long Mrs. Morrison returned, carrying the large tin can of used tea leaves. "Your mother told me if I scatter them about the floor when I sweep, it will help keep down the dust."

I bet she didn't tell you where we are going, Michiko thought. These days her mother's face was expressionless. Her pale, thin lips pressed together so tightly they almost disappeared. She cleaned the house from top to bottom, took down the curtains, and moved the furniture. Michiko knew her mother was not happy about moving to Japan.

"Why don't you come with me to the church," Mrs. Morrison suggested. "The flower beds could do with a weeding before the wedding." She giggled at what she said.

~ ~ ~

When they arrived at the church, Mabel, in a large cotton apron with a knotted tea towel about her head, appeared in the doorway. "Do we take everything off the notice board as well?" she asked.

Edna replied, "Michiko can do the notice board. Clarence, you tackle the dandelions."

Michiko dropped her rake onto the grass. She entered to the sound of Mabel pumping the carpeted pedals, making the old organ wheeze out the wedding march.

The notice board was so full it was a wonder anyone noticed anything. An unclaimed mitten from last winter covered some of the messages and announcements. Michiko decided to remove everything, throw out what was out of date, and rearrange.

Along with the usual notices of choir practices, upcoming events, and club meetings was a small newspaper clipping. It was so small the brass thumbtack holding it up covered most of it. She pried back the tack and read.

> *Family Wanted: Owners of gladiola farm need help with business and household. Man required. Must be able to operate tractor, harvest and sort bulbs, sell flowers.*

Woman needed for housework and meals. Small house included. Will accept Asian family. Write for details.

Michiko stared at what she held in her hand. She turned it over to see if there was a date. All that it said on back was, "Raspberry Jam — 24 oz jar — 29 cents with two preserves coupons."

How long had this ad been here? Michiko asked herself. The paper wasn't yellow or faded. How many other Japanese families had read it? Taking a deep breath, Michiko folded the tiny strip of words and slipped it into her blouse pocket. *This just might be the answer to my prayers.*

Chapter Twenty-Four

THE WEDDING

Mrs. Morrison's rickety camera had a lever that kept on getting stuck. "I hope this doesn't make the pictures blurry," Mr. Hayashi mumbled.

Sadie Minagawa and Kaz Katsumoto celebrated their wedding in Mrs. Morrison's back garden. Dark orange lilies bobbed along the fence. Roses filled the air with their sweet perfume. The huge lilac tree by the gate wore a white bow around its trunk.

Sadie made an enchanting bride in her white satin dress. Michiko's mother laboured many nights after the baby slept, stitching tiny pearl buttons along the neck. Her white high-heel shoes came from the catalogue courtesy of the female teachers. "It's an investment," Sadie told everyone with a laugh "They all hope to use them some day." She smiled down at her huge bouquet of field daisies and wild ferns tied with a white ribbon.

Michiko wore a borrowed dress of yellow chiffon with short puffy sleeves, too small for one of the teachers. Her satin hair band, a present from Mrs. Morrison, shone against her shiny bobbed hair. She couldn't stop pointing her legs to admire her new snow-white knee socks and black patent shoes.

Mr. Hayashi made sure all the men at the wedding wore suits, but the groom surprised them all. When Mr. Katsumoto arrived he took everyone's breath away. Dressed in grey-and-white-striped pants and a black coat with tails, he looked like a diplomat. "It was a gift from my team, when I went to Japan," he said with a grin. "All baseball stars had to dress properly."

~ ~ ~

The wedding banquet sat on a long trestle of sheeted planks in the backyard. Tall silver-plated candelabras stood in the middle. Roses bowed from jam jars. There were china plates and silver forks. Beside the huge platters of chicken were large bowls of potato salad, coleslaw, and sliced tomatoes. Glass dishes of pickled beets and deviled eggs sat on either side of enormous two-storey loaves of bread.

But most amazing of all was the three-tiered wedding cake. Mrs. Morrison got every one of her friends to save sugar so she could bake and ice a proper wedding cake. It looked beautiful, but only the top layer was cake.

"Who will know in the pictures?" beamed Mrs. Morrison. She pinned brown paper strips cut from grocery bags around two hatboxes and iced them as if they were cake. Michiko would get to scrape the iced paper later.

"Those flowers look real," Clarence said. He was dressed in a hand-me-down suit from his oldest brother, and smelled of the soap they sold at the drugstore.

"They are real," Michiko said. She helped Mrs. Morrison hold each of the pansy blossoms with tweezers while she brushed egg white across the petals. Then they sprinkled them with fine sugar and let them dry. "But you can still eat them," Michiko assured him.

The sound of a large truck lumbering down the lane made everyone stop chattering and look up. Ted's lumber truck flowed with white streamers. Two wooden boxes draped in a white sheet took the place of the logs.

"Your bridal carriage awaits you," he announced from the cab. He was taking them back to the hotel. All the teachers bunked in with someone from the orchard to give them privacy. As they climbed into the truck, the teachers flung confetti. Hiro tried to fill his pockets with what he found on the ground.

Eiko stepped up to kiss the bride.

As she waved goodbye, Michiko's only wish was that her grandfather had been there. But she stopped herself from thinking about it. Today Sadie would agree with him when he said, *"We can never see the sun rise by looking to the west."*

"Before you leave," Edna Morrison said as she removed her new flowered hat, "there's a letter here for you."

"A letter for me?" questioned Michiko's mother. "A letter came here for me?"

"It's on the mantelpiece," Edna said. "Bring the baby inside and read it."

Michiko ran to the baby carriage. "I'll bring her," she said.

Little bristles of fear filled her chest. In a way Michiko had told a lie, pretending she was her mother when she wrote the letter to the poster of the ad she'd found on the church bulletin board. But her little sister, like herself and Hiro, was Canadian. She shouldn't grow up in Japan. She prayed her mother would understand.

~ ~ ~

That night, Eiko held out the letter to Sam. "Read it yourself," she said.

He ignored her and walked out of the room.

Michiko's mother followed him, waving the letter in her hand.

"According to this," she said, "we would live for free in a small farmhouse that has electricity, hot water, and a bathroom."

Her father said nothing.

"You will work in a garden, just like you do now, only growing flowers. You will also help with sales, like you do now. I will cook and clean, just like I do now."

"Our rent will be free in Japan," he said in a low voice.

"A house for a family is included," she said. "They are willing to pay you $6.00 a week," Eiko continued, "and I get a salary as well."

Sam looked Eiko in the eye and took the letter from her hand. His chocolate eyes grew cold and stale. "I don't know how to drive a tractor," he complained after reading it.

"You know how to drive a car and a delivery truck, how can it be that much different?"

Michiko knew her mother had made a lot of good points.

"What are we going to do for travelling money?" asked her father. "There are five of us."

Michiko couldn't stay quiet any longer. "I know!" she shouted in her eagerness to solve this new problem. "We can ask Mrs. Morrison to lend us the money."

The force with which her father slammed his fist on the table startled her. "Don't you ever suggest that again," he said in a deep firm voice. He stomped downstairs.

Michiko didn't understand his reaction. It couldn't possibly be because Edna Morrison was *hakujin*. Maybe it was one of those old-fashioned Japanese things her mother and Aunt Sadie always talked about. Maybe a man could never borrow money from a woman.

Her mother shook her head at Michiko, as if saying, "I told you so."

"I thought it was a good idea," she murmured. "Why won't he accept help?"

"Your father is a proud man," her mother said. "He would never borrow."

"We would pay it all back," Michiko said.

"There has to be another way," was all her mother said. "We have some time. They said they have help for the flowers but not for the bulbs. If we want the position, we will have to be there by September."

Life went on as usual. Each morning Michiko made breakfast for her brother. She tidied the kitchen before she went to school. At noon she came home to help with the routines of the household. Monday was washing day; Tuesday, ironing. They baked on Wednesday. Thursday was for sewing and knitting, although now her mother only made minor repairs of their clothes. There was no time with the new baby to take in work from other people. Friday was for the garden. Saturday was for the bathhouse, and Sunday, church.

"Mrs. Morrison said she wanted her house painted," Michiko told her father after church one day. "Do you think Uncle Ted would be able to fit it in?"

"That's much too big a job for weekend work," her father answered. "Ted's working hard with the lumber company. He needs his weekends to rest."

"Maybe Clarence and I could do it?" Michiko suggested. "He's looking for work."

"What if I helped too?" her mother added.

"Paint a house?" Sam looked at his wife in disbelief.

"No, silly," she replied. "I could watch the store while the three of you paint. Mrs. Morrison would love to entertain Hiro. The baby would be fine in her carriage in the store."

"It would be a way of making money," her father said tapping his finger to his chin. "I'll have to see what she says."

By the end of the week they had a plan. Eiko would mind the shop in the morning. Sam, Michiko, and Clarence would paint in the morning, while it was cool. Mrs. Morrison borrowed a cot from the church and set it up on the back verandah for Hiro. While he napped, Michiko and Clarence would clean the brushes and eat their lunch. Sam would come home for lunch and work in the drugstore.

Mrs. Morrison lent Michiko her alarm clock and showed her how to use it. As she wound the tiny key at the back, Michiko thought how there was never a need for an alarm clock when they were living at the farmhouse. The morning started with the noise of the draft creaking open, the scrape of the metal shovel and the clatter of wood going into the stove.

They would work for $1.75 a day. Clarence would take home fifty cents. The rest would go into Geechan's thin wooden box with the white owl on the front.

Michiko's mother made a few small changes in the store, adding baby toys and ladies' magazines. When Sam came home for lunch the store was often crowded with women, playing with the baby and making small purchases.

"You are good for business," Sam said taking the baby into his arms. "Time to think about giving you a name."

"When are we going to have the baby's christening?" Michiko asked at dinner that night. She already had a long list of possible names for her tiny new sister. "She has to be called something."

"It all depends on where we are going," was her mother's reply. She looked long and hard at Sam. "Her name must suit her life."

Chapter Twenty-Five

HANNAH

Each night after dinner, her father counted the money in Geechan's cigar box. Her mother counted it a second time, *dame ohsi*. Bert was so impressed by the job they did on Mrs. Morrison's house he asked them to paint his barn. Her father upped the price and Bert agreed.

"Two dollars a day makes Japan far away," Michiko told herself each night as she crossed out a day on her calendar. But she never said it out loud. She didn't want to offend.

Mr. Hayashi visited that night. Moving out of town wasn't as easy as Michiko thought. Mr. Hayashi had to write to the Security Commission, telling them her father had a job and accommodations for his family in Oakville. Then her father had to take the letter from Oakville to the RCMP office down the street. Mr. Hayashi told them that they weren't giving out anymore permits to Toronto, but they might for Oakville. No one had applied to Oakville.

"What about the other papers?" her mother asked in a hushed voice.

Her father shrugged.

A strange chill went through Michiko's mind when she saw that shrug. Did it mean Mr. Hayashi's set of papers didn't matter, or moving to Oakville didn't matter? But the strangest thing of all was that her mother insisted no one know of their plans, not even Uncle Ted, Auntie Sadie, or Uncle Kaz.

Michiko had a hard time calling her teacher Uncle Kaz. At least Raymond and the rest of the boys in her class finally stopped asking her how it felt to have such a famous person in her family. Her mother said everything was to remain the same until all was arranged. That meant at school and everywhere else. It was getting difficult for Michiko to keep such a big secret.

"The Minagawa baby is two months old," Aunt Sadie said one day at church. "I'm on my second name and she doesn't even have her first."

Michiko's mother smiled. "*Obon*," she said, "is when we will name her."

"What is an *Obon*?" asked Clarence when she told him the christening was August 15.

"*Obon* isn't a thing," Michiko replied. "It's a kind of holiday."

"What kind of things do you do?"

Michiko shrugged. She wished her Geechan was around. He knew all about the festivals of the Japanese Buddhists. She was going to have to ask someone else about this. She knew exactly who it would be, if she could find the courage to ask.

"Do you want to go to the orchard with me?" Michiko asked Clarence as they laid the paint brushes in the sun to dry.

"Who are you going to see?" he asked. Michiko hadn't been there since Kiko left.

Michiko took a deep breath. "I want to see Mr. Yama," she said.

Clarence opened his mouth and shut it. He reminded Michiko of a goldfish she once had. "Mr. Yama?" he screeched. "Why do you want to visit that guy?"

"You just asked me about *Obon*," Michiko said. "Mr. Yama could tell us."

"Well he won't talk to you if I go along," Clarence said. "I'm *hi-coo-jean*."

"Maybe we should ask George to come along," Michiko said with a smile.

Clarence opened and closed his mouth a second time. "Are you crazy?"

"All Japs are crazy," Michiko replied. "Let's go find George."

Even though he had the best bike in town, George was never far from home. They spotted him pumping his tires on the front lawn.

"We can't just walk up to him," Clarence said. "His mother will call him inside."

"I'll go on ahead," Michiko said with a smile. "You can do something else with him."

"He'll want to know what," Clarence said.

"Tell him he needs to learn how to throw a baseball," Michiko said.

"I don't know," Clarence said removing his cap and running his fingers through his hair.

"See you later," Michiko said. She turned and walked away. Maybe, just maybe, they could learn to get along. Clarence and George might even become friends.

On Mr. Yama's wooden steps Michiko learned all about the Feast of Lanterns.

"People stop work," Mr. Yama told her in broken English. "Everyone go home."

"What do they do with the lanterns?" Michiko asked.

"Lanterns go outside house," he said. He put up his brown leathery hand to shade his eyes and look around. Just like her grandfather, Mr. Yama used his hands to explain what he meant. "Family spirits see lanterns and find way home." He rubbed his stomach. "Then family have big feast and put food for spirit guests too."

"Then what happens?" Michiko prompted.

The old man blinked. "People take lanterns to water," he said. He swayed his body from side to side. "They have big dance to say goodbye." He moved his hands up and down in front of him making waves. "Lanterns go on water so spirits find way back."

Michiko looked at the man with the purple blotch on his face and sighed. He may not be beautiful on the outside, she thought, but he had beauty inside. "You know, Mr. Yama," she said, getting up, "I think the people in the orchard should celebrate Obon." She dusted off her shorts. "After all, we have a lake and a river."

The old man blinked as if he saw her for the first time.

~ ~ ~

"I didn't have to get the papers back," Mr. Hayashi told Michiko's parents that night. "I never sent them in. I needed two signatures. Remember, we were interrupted by the baby."

Michiko's mother let out a squeal and threw her arms around the surprised security officer. "That is wonderful news," she told him. Then she did the unthinkable. She kissed him on the cheek.

"Are we good to go?" her father asked.

"If you've got the money," Mr. Hayashi said, "I'll apply for your tickets tomorrow."

Michiko's hands went to her mouth. All their papers were in order. Tomorrow they could buy their train tickets and they could move to Ontario. She clapped her hands. Hiro copied.

A small cry came from the carriage. Michiko looked at the small fist waving in the air. "That's right, baby sister," she said rushing to her side. "You can give a cheer. Because of you, you will be growing up in Ontario."

Michiko's mother lifted the baby from the carriage. "So, Hannah," she said, "are you ready to wear your pretty white christening dress?"

"Hana?" Michiko and her father repeated together. "We are calling her Hana?"

"Hana is a Japanese name," Sam said.

"I thought it was a Canadian name," Michiko said.

"It's both," said her mother. "And it is the middle name of her soon-to-be godmother."

"Well, what do you know," Michiko's father said. "Our baby girl is a flower after all."

"Edna Hannah Morrison," Michiko said. "I never knew."

~ ~ ~

A slight breeze swept across the cemetery slope, scattering the fallen leaves. Michiko carried the spade. She stepped across the grass, careful not to tread on anyone's bones. Her mother, father, and aunt walked together. Mrs. Morrison held Hiro's hand. Uncle Kaz pushed the baby carriage. Uncle Ted carried a small tree in a pot.

Michiko watched her mother brush the leaves from the rough slab of pebbly cement. Her light touch reminded Michiko of the way she soothed Geechan's brow in the hospital. Her father, Uncle Ted, and Uncle Kaz pulled out weeds from around the flat stone. Sadie patted the stone as if she were making rice balls. Ted dug a hole and put the cherry tree into place.

In her dream the night before, Michiko walked through the long grassy field of the farmhouse. Her grandfather stood against the blue sky, waving. The orchard was pink with cherry trees. She ran toward him and their fingers touched. She woke up right then and lay in bed, knowing that he would always be with them.

Everyone drew together, holding hands around the tree. They bowed their heads and prayed in silence. Even Hiro remained quiet. The smell of the weedy grass reminded Michiko of sitting in the field with her grandfather, waiting to catch fireflies. She made up her mind to do that with Hiro. That is, if there were fireflies in Oakville.

Japanese Vocabulary
in order of appearance in story

origami	Japanese art of paper folding
cha	green tea
yancha	naughty
Geechan	Grandfather
kairanban	homemade newspaper or bulletin
Kanji	Japanese alphabet letters
shoyu	soya sauce
ofuro	Japanese public bath
"Ashi o kiosukete kudasai"	"Take care of your feet"
haikara	too good for the neighbourhood

"Yancha kozo de ne" "Such a mischievous kid"

furoshiki	bundle made by tying four corners of a square cloth
miso	red or white bean paste
tamago yaki	omelette
Asahi	famous Japanese-Canadian baseball team
kanemochi	upper class, people with money
gangara	hold on, keep going, persevere
Ara!	Watch Out!
hakujin	Caucasian, or white person
haiseki	discrimination, prejudice
batsu	Japanese gesture of crossing arms to mean no
ki-chigai geechan	crazy old man
baka	stupid
konnichiwa	hello

tatami	Japanese straw floor mat
Yamoto Damashii	True Spirit of Japan
sayonara	goodbye
Sode Boshi	Kimono Sleeve in the Sky Constellation
sumi	solid rectangular stick of ink
suzuri	ink stone for grinding stick into water
fude	Oriental paint brush
kami	Japanese painting paper
chokuhitsu	Basic *sumi-e* stroke — vertical brush stroke
sokuhitsu	Basic *sumi-e* stroke — slanted brush stroke
hatusyume	the new year
geta	high wooden shoes with thongs
Ikebana	Japanese flower arranging
Haiku	type of Japanese poetry

"Najii des'ka?"   "Do you have a watch?"

majnai   trick that brings good fortune

Haru Matsura   Spring Flower Festival

hanten   housecoat

sakura   cherry blossom

taiko   drum

niwatori   chickens

dame ohsi   second time — to make sure

Obon   Buddhist Lantern Festival

Author's Note

Growing up, I knew nothing of the treatment of Japanese Canadians during the Second World War. History books concealed how the government left them penniless, homeless, and without a future. My admiration goes out to all the brave Japanese-Canadian men and women who kept their families fed, clothed, and educated without funds or bitterness.

Mrs. Morrison, Clarence, George, and the rest of the townspeople are fictional. The names of the Japanese families are changed, but the people involved are real. My mother-in-law, Eiko Kitagawa Maruno, allowed me to explore her life through photographs and memories. To see their life in the ghost town, my husband and I travelled to the Kootenays to visit the Japanese Memorial Centre in New Denver. Thanks to Noburo Hayashi, caretaker and interpreter, who helped us find Nelson Farm and the original railway tracks.

I am grateful to Sylvia McConnell for accepting my first manuscript, *When the Cherry Blossoms Fell*, which began the Cherry Blossom series. Thanks go to the team at Dundurn for continuing the story of Michiko and her family.

To my avid readers, Susan Onn, Nancy Wannamaker, and Brenda Julie, thank you for asking the right questions and being part of my later-life career as an author.

To Stan, my husband, David and Erin, my children, and my friend Anne More, thank you for your never-ending support and encouragement.

When the Cherry Blossoms Fell
A Cherry Blossom Book
978-1-894917834
$9.95

Nine-year-old Michiko Minagawa bids her father goodbye before her birthday celebration. She doesn't know the government has ordered all Japanese-born men out of the province. Ten days later, her family joins hundreds of Japanese-Canadians on a train to the interior of British Columbia. Even though her Aunt Sadie jokes about it, they have truly reached the "Land of No." There are no paved roads, no streetlights, and no streetcars. The house in which they are to live is dirty and drafty. At school Michiko learns the truth of her situation. She must face local prejudice, the worst winter in forty years, and her first Christmas without her father.

DUNDURN
www.dundurn.com

VISIT US AT
Dundurn.com
Definingcanada.ca
@dundurnpress
Facebook.com/dundurnpress

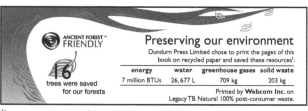